her every day. And now she was bringing hope into his life by agreeing to have his baby. *Their* baby.

He put down his fork and reached for her small hand. 'You won't change your mind, will you, Chantal?' he said huskily.

She felt the warmth of his hand around hers and skin against skin seemed almost erotic. She could feel deep down that being with Michel was affecting her more than it should.

'No, of course I won't change my mind.' She stood up. 'Dessert?' she asked briskly.

He could feel something like an electric current running between them. Inside him was a powerful feeling of wanting to take Chantal in his arms and hold her until the feeling went away. He stood up and put his arms around her, drawing her close. This didn't make sense. She should be pushing him away, telling him to stick to the plan. He bent his head to kiss her.

She parted her lips as every sense in her body ignited with passion and longing. She was feeling overwhelmed by the sensual fluidity of her body as she moulded herself against Michel's hard, virile, muscular frame. She was melting away as he held her tightly. There was a powerful force gripping her. She didn't even want to stir in his arms in case the dream ended.

He lifted her into his arms, carrying her towards the door. The   need for words as he carried her upstairs.   ng in to the
mag   y his
acti   is to
ban

Dear Reader

I've returned once more to my favourite part of France for the setting of HER MIRACLE TWINS. I fell in love with the area when I strolled hand in hand one summer's day along a favourite beach with my boyfriend, John, who was soon to be my husband. Later we took our children. Now some of our children and grandchildren live not far from this beach.

I still walk along the same beach if I'm searching for a new romantic story. Although my husband died a few years ago I still feel the inspiration he used to give me when I needed to conjure up a romantic hero.

The beach is set in a beautiful area of hills and valleys near fashionable Le Touquet and the picturesque old town of Montreuil-sur-Mer. It's a perfect background for the romance of Chantal and Michel. In HER MIRACLE TWINS we also meet up again with Chantal's cousin Julia and her husband, Bernard, who were the hero and heroine in SUMMER WITH A FRENCH SURGEON. Chantal, like her cousin Julia, has many emotional obstacles to overcome before she finds true love and happiness.

I hope you enjoy reading this romantic story as much as I enjoyed writing it.

Margaret

HER
MIRACLE TWINS

BY
MARGARET BARKER

Published in Great Britain 2014
by Mills & Boon, an imprint of Harlequin (UK) Limited,
Eton House, 18-24 Paradise Road, Richmond, Surrey, TW9 1SR

© 2014 Margaret Barker

ISBN: 978 0 263 90742 1

Margaret Barker has enjoyed a variety of interesting careers. A State Registered Nurse and qualified teacher, she holds a degree in French and Linguistics, and is a Licentiate of the Royal Academy of Music. As a full-time writer, Margaret says, 'Writing is my most interesting career, because it fits perfectly into family life. Sadly, my husband died of cancer in 2006, but I still live in our idyllic sixteenth-century house near the East Anglian coast. Our grown-up children have flown the nest, but they often fly back again, bringing their own young families with them for wonderful weekend and holiday reunions.'

Recent titles by the same author:

SUMMER WITH A FRENCH SURGEON
A FATHER FOR BABY ROSE
GREEK DOCTOR CLAIMS HIS BRIDE
THE FATHERHOOD MIRACLE

**These books are also available in eBook format
from www.millsandboon.co.uk**

To John, my inspiration always.

CHAPTER ONE

'IT WAS THAT wretched stone just under the surface that tripped me up, Michel. Look at that dreadful, jagged monster. Somebody must have—'

'Chantal, keep still, will you? I'm trying to assess how much damage you've done.'

'Damage I've done? I'm trying to keep still but— Ow, that hurt!'

Sprawled on the sand, Chantal glared up at the tall, athletic man in white running shorts and black tee shirt who was now kneeling on the sand beside her. He appeared to have come from nowhere as she'd tripped and hurt her ankle. She deduced he must have been running behind her, but he was barely recognisable as the suave director of Accident and Emergency she was used to seeing as she worked alongside him at the Hôpital de la Plage.

'If you weren't my boss I'd...'

He looked down at her, smiling in the most patronisingly irritating yet surprisingly sexy way, his fingers firmly supporting her swelling ankle. She told herself to concentrate on the pain, which would help her to stop fantasising about something that was never going to happen to her again—especially with the usually serious, work-focussed Dr Michel Devine.

'I'm going to have to carry you up the beach to my car up there on the promenade so I can get you back to the hospital.'

'No! I don't want to be carried. Just help me to my feet so I can hop as far as—'

'Be quiet, Dr Winstone, and that's an order!'

She frowned as she decided to give in to him. He always got his own way in Urgences but she'd never seen him quite so domineering before. She couldn't help admiring the expression on his face. It made him appear even more desirable as a man. And she didn't do desirable any more. Not since last September.

She decided the pain was addling her brain, filling her head full of mad ideas. Weird feelings she would never have contemplated since she'd changed completely on that awful night.

Effortlessly, Michel picked her up and carried her in his arms across the sand. The pain in her ankle was now becoming more intense. She decided to give in completely. He was, after all, the most experienced expert in accidental injuries for miles around, probably in the whole of France. And it was a good feeling to simply relax in his arms.

Yes, she should be grateful he'd come along when he had. And the pleasant feeling of strong, muscular, masculine arms around her helped to counteract the pain. Since the two-timing Jacques had done the dirty on her she'd never expected to tolerate a man's arms around her again.

As he was loading her into the back seat of his car she put on a contrite tone of voice and told him she was sorry.

'Sorry for what? Being a difficult patient? Forget it. I

get to see them every day. Once I've shown them how to co-operate, as I did with you, we get on fine. Your child-ish behaviour was because you were suffering from shock, probably still are.'

He was looking directly into her eyes now, an expres-sion of concentration creasing his forehead. She found herself admiring his warm, brown, expressive eyes.

'How's the pain now? Worse?'

She nodded as a particularly sharp spasm passed through her ankle. 'Mmm. Do you have any—?'

He was already pulling out a strip of painkillers from his glove compartment. 'Swallow those two with this water.' He opened a new pack. 'Now, try to keep the ankle as still as you can. I'll get it X-rayed as soon as we get back to hospital.'

She lay still as Michel drove off. The welcome sight of the Hôpital de la Plage came into view and she gave a sigh of relief.

'It was the warm spring sunshine that tempted me out this Sunday morning,' she muttered, almost to herself, as Michel drove up to the front entrance of the hospital. 'I should have stayed in bed.'

'So should I. I hadn't planned that I would have to work on my day off.'

He switched off the engine as a porter arrived to re-monstrate with the owner of this car parking in an am-bulance space.

'Oh, sorry, Dr Devine. I hadn't recognised you. I see you've got a patient on the back seat so— Oh, it's you, Dr Winstone. Are you all right?'

'No, she's not all right. Could you please bring a stretcher and then park my car in the staff car park?'

Chantal could tell that Michel was reverting to type

after his initial attempt to be patient with her. She remained very still and quiet as a nurse came out to help the porter load her onto the trolley. Michel supervised while holding her right ankle to prevent any further damage as they trundled along to X-Ray.

'Good news No fractures.' Michel was pointing out the X-rays illuminated on the screen.

She raised her head from the pillow.

'Thank heavens for that. So it's simply a sprain. I'll get the ankle strapped up and I'll be on duty again tomorrow morning.'

He frowned. 'Chantal, there's nothing simple about a sprain, as you well know. I think you've been lucky that you haven't torn the surrounding ligaments but there's been mild stretching of the ligaments which will have to be dealt with. The treatment is to minimise the pain. You've started on the paracetamol. Two five hundred mg every six hours will take the edge off it. For the first three days you need complete rest, ice-pack applications pressed on to the injury for fifteen minutes every two hours and—'

'Michel, I can't possibly do all that. I've got too much to do.'

'Exactly. That's why I'm going to put you in a side ward attached to Female Orthopaedic. I take no chances with my staff. Deal with a sprain properly at the beginning and future problems shouldn't arise.'

Chantal lay back on the trolley, looking up at the bright lights above her head. Michel was on the phone to the orthopaedic sister. He was smiling now. 'Yes, we're coming along now if that's OK with you, Sidonie? Good. Yes, you know Chantal, Dr Winstone. She's been with us in

Emergency since February. We'll go over the treatment she needs when I arrive. I've got hold of a porter at last. Be with you in a couple of minutes.'

Half an hour later Chantal was safely settled in an orthopaedic bed, wearing the most unglamorous hospital pyjamas. Her right leg was elevated on hard orthopaedic cushions, Sister Sidonie was applying an ice pack to the painful area. Michel was watching her every move as if ready to criticise.

'Ow!' Chantal found it impossible to check her cry as Sister pressed on the painful area.

Michel was nodding his approval. 'That's exactly right, Sister. More pressure on the injury just there. Keep it like that for fifteen minutes. Here, let me show you the exact pressure required to reduce this inflammation.'

Taking over from Sister Sidonie, he placed his fingers on Chantal's ankle.

'Michel!'

'Yes, I expect that did hurt a bit but you'll thank me for this later.'

Chantal lay back against the pillows and gave in. She didn't know what he had in mind for the thanks she would have to give him. Even through the pain he was inflicting she got a thrill at the touch of his fingers. Most bizarre. She'd worked with this man for over two months and hadn't ever thought of him in this way. As she'd suspected earlier, the pain must have addled her brain. She'd gone back to childhood days and was imagining he was a knight in shining armour who'd come to rescue her from danger, probably on a white horse instead of simply jogging along the beach.

'That's better.' He smiled and patted her hand.

His teeth were very white, she noticed now, very even.

His dark hair, which was hanging down over his forehead as he leaned over her, gave him a rumpled, little-boy look, something she'd never seen before as he worked efficiently on his patients. But it was those sexy dark brown eyes that were impossibly attractive. How come they hadn't registered with her until this morning?

'Sister, I'll be back later in the day. Reapply the pack for fifteen minutes every two hours. In about four days we'll be able to put the ankle in a tubular compression bandage and get the physiotherapist to introduce massage, ultrasound therapy and gentle joint movement.'

Chantal raise her head. 'Michel, when can I go back to my room in the medics' quarters?'

'That will depend on your progress. Hopefully in a few days we should be able to get you up on crutches. Once you can move around with the use of a stick I might let you go back to your room so long as you don't take any weight on the right ankle. You may even spend an hour or so in Emergency doing paperwork or something non-strenuous. We'll have to see how you get on.'

She couldn't help noticing that he'd reverted to his totally professional manner with her. She was just another patient requiring attention on his day off. Fine. He was just another medical colleague. When these unusual flights of fancy left her she would revert to type as well.

He was glancing at his watch. 'Any questions before I have to go?'

She suddenly felt a moment of panic. 'When will you be coming back?' As soon as she'd asked the pathetic question she regretted it. What was the matter with her? The pain gave her an excuse perhaps but she hoped he didn't read anything into it.

Sidonie was smiling at her in a reassuring, almost maternal way. 'It's OK, Chantal, we'll take care of you.'

'I'll be back this evening. Don't worry. A month from now you'll wonder what all the fuss was about.'

She certainly would. As she watched the lithe, athletic figure disappear through the door she was experiencing mixed emotions. Somehow she felt she was getting to know the real person beneath the dour façade Michel presented to his professional colleagues. Her emotions this morning were dangerously out of order. She too had always elected to present a façade to her colleagues to cover up the agony she'd been through before she'd started working here.

Sidonie applied more pressure with the ice pack. 'Quite a charmer, isn't he?'

Chantal hesitated. 'Well, I wouldn't say that. He's good at his job.'

'Oh, he's devoted to his job. You know his wife died don't you? Over three years ago, I believe. Apparently, she died of cancer and he's never got over it. We all fancied him when he arrived to be Director of Emergency, over a year ago now.'

Sidonie gave an expressive sigh. 'Well, who wouldn't fancy him? Tall, dark and handsome and built like an athlete. But he made it quite clear to all of us that he wasn't interested in relationships. He's the sort of man who obviously adored his wife and will never take a long-term girlfriend. Definitely not remarry, that's for sure! She must have been a very special woman to deserve such loyalty from him.'

Sidonie paused in her observations and gave another sigh. 'That's unfortunate for all the unmarried staff who lavish attention on him. If I wasn't a forty-year-old married woman with two children I'd fancy him myself.'

She removed the ice pack and smiled down at her patient. 'You've been working in Emergency since Feb-

ruary, haven't you? I heard you were on the medical staff
of a hospital in Paris before you came here. How does the
Hôpital de la Plage compare to your previous hospital?'

Chantal hesitated. 'Well, it's different. Actually, it's
like coming home for me. You see, I was born just a few
miles away in Montreuil. My English father died when
I was seven. My French mother resumed her teaching
career after that and she took me to live in Paris where
she'd got a job. That's where she brought me up, although
we always used to return to this area and stay here during the long summer vacation.

'This coastline feels like my second home because I
know it so well. When I was old enough I did my medical training in Paris and took a staff position when I
qualified.'

Sidonie put the ice pack down on a trolley and sat
down beside her patient. 'Was it because you regard this
area as your second home that you chose to leave Paris?'

Chantal looked at the figure of the kindly woman and
found her experienced presence very comforting. She
welcomed a girly chat to take her mind off the pain and
the unexpected turn of events today.

She lay back against her pillows. 'It was a sudden decision. Very sudden.'

She drew in her breath as the awful memory of that
fateful day flooded back to her.

'One minute I was on cloud nine, in love with the man
of my dreams, three months pregnant with his much-
wanted baby.'

She hesitated. Should she, indeed could she, go on?
What did she have to lose?

'Then the phone rang and everything changed.'

Her voice was quavering as she gathered her thoughts.

Was it really a good idea to unload the sordid details onto someone who was a colleague?

The orthopaedic sister was watching her with a deeply sympathetic expression on her face, as if anticipating what was to come. Oh, it would be good for her to get it off her chest. She'd bottled it up ever since she arrived at the Hôpital de la Plage. It was about time she relaxed and socialised a bit more. It wasn't her fault she'd been totally hoodwinked by a despicable, two-timing scoundrel.

She could hear the sound of a heavy trolley being pushed past her door through the swing doors into the ward and the murmur of the nurses and patients as the doors opened.

A nurse knocked, before opening her door. 'Dr Winstone, would you like some lunch?'

Chantal shook her head. 'No, thank you, Nurse.'

Sidonie turned her head. 'Is everything OK in the ward, Sylvie?'

The young nurse smiled. 'Fine, Sister. A nice quiet Sunday for once.'

'I'll be back to check the medicines after you've served the lunch. Pay attention to the patients on extra fluids, won't you?'

'Of course, Sister.' She turned back to her patient. 'So what happened after the phone rang?'

Chantal moved her good foot into a more comfortable position at the side of the cushions supporting her injured ankle as that fateful evening last September came flooding back.

'I was in the kitchen in my apartment, roasting a chicken for our supper, I remember. My boyfriend had phoned earlier to invite himself round that evening so I'd picked up a chicken at the supermarket on my way home from hospital.'

She swallowed hard. 'The phone rang. I answered it. It was a woman's voice. She asked if Jacques was there. I called him over and went on preparing the meal. I assumed it was probably one of his private patients. He seemed to have lots of those. He was such a charming person. Unpredictable, though. I never knew when he was going to turn up.'

Already she could feel the bitterness welling up inside her. 'He took the phone into the sitting room. I could hear his voice, very low, more like a whisper. Then suddenly he started shouting. 'No, you mustn't do that! No, you can't come here. You can't!'

Sidonie sat very still as she waited for Chantal to continue. She could see how upset she was.

'He slammed down the phone and came back into the kitchen. His face was drained of all colour and he was trembling. At the same time I could hear footsteps on the stairs coming up from the ground floor of my apartment block. Then hammering on the door.'

'Who was it?'

'His wife. I had no idea he was married. It transpired that she'd been caring for her sick mother in the south of France for a few months. A friend had tipped her off that her husband was being unfaithful and had given her my address and phone number.'

'So what happened when his wife arrived?'

Chantal cleared her throat. 'She started shrieking at him. Hitting him in the chest with her fists. He grabbed her wrists, fending off the blows as he tried to placate her. He said he could explain everything. How pathetic! The evidence was there before the poor woman's eyes, for heaven's sake. I found myself feeling sorry for her.'

'So, did she start shouting at you?'

'No, that was the strange thing. She barely glanced

at me. It was her pig of a husband she was mad with. I'd
heard enough about his womanising as she continued to
hurl abuse at him. I just wanted it all to stop. So I opened
my door and asked them both to leave.'

'And then?'

'They noticed me at last. His wife grabbed his arm
and pulled him towards the door. I continued to hold the
door wide open. She was still shouting. I told them both
again to get out of my apartment. After they'd gone I went
into my bedroom. My brain had gone numb. I lay down
on the bed and closed my eyes, willing myself to sleep.'

No, she couldn't tell her any more of the agony that
had come afterwards, not now anyway. She wanted to
move forward with her life. She was a different person
from the innocent, trusting woman she'd been. The heart-
breaking experience later that night had changed her for
ever. She couldn't even speak about her miscarriage.

'I'm sorry, Sidonie, to burden you with all this.'

Sidonie leaned across and patted her hand. 'Thank
you for sharing a confidence with me. I feel privileged
to have been told something of your background. You
always seemed so quiet and withdrawn when you first
started working in Emergency. I hadn't realised the suffering you'd been through. If ever you need a shoulder
to cry on...'

'Thanks, but I've done all the crying I'm going to do.
The past is over. It's the present and the future that are
important to me now.'

She must have fallen asleep after Sister had gone back
into the ward. The sun, which had been shining full into
her window, had dipped below the rooftops of the hospital. She became aware of someone being in the room
and turned to look at her bedside chair.

'I hope I didn't wake you?'

'Julia! What a lovely surprise.' She held out her arms at the sight of her cousin then winced as she unwittingly moved her damaged ankle.

Julia rose to her feet. 'Don't try to move, Chantal.' She bent down and kissed her cheek. You looked so peaceful when I came in. Sister said you would probably be waking up soon.'

'Oh, it's so good to see you again. How did you know I was here?'

'Well, Bernard phoned Sidonie this afternoon to say he was coming in to Orthopaedics to check on the patient he'd chosen for teaching purposes tomorrow morning. Bernard always asks their permission, checks these patients carefully and makes sure they know that he will be supervising his students all the time. I remember when I was one of his students I was always so impressed with the care he took to ensure the patients knew exactly what they were letting themselves in for.'

'I love to hear about when you were one of Bernard's students and you found him so difficult and demanding as a professor while you were studying with him for that prestigious exam in orthopaedic surgery.'

Julia laughed. 'He was only being difficult, he told me afterwards, to ensure I got the best results. After that I managed to thaw him out and...well, you know how it all ended. Marriage and a baby on the way. Anyway, Sister Sidonie told Bernard you were in the side ward here, having sprained your ankle and stretched the ligaments. That must be really painful. I just had to come and check how you are and if there was anything you need.'

'I can't fault the way they've treated me. Right from the time Michel picked me up off the beach'

'Michel? What on earth were the two of you doing on the beach together?'

Chantal, well aware of the insinuating grin on her cousin's face, quickly set her straight with the basic details, starting with the important fact that they hadn't gone to the beach together. Michel had arrived just as she'd tripped up on a killer of a stone absolutely lying in wait for her.

'Ah, I see. So Michel brought you back to hospital, set up your treatment and then disappeared.'

'He's coming back this evening to check on me. How's young Philippe?'

Julia's expression softened. It was always obvious that she adored her husband's son from his first marriage.

'He's fine. Marianne—you remember our brilliant housekeeper who's been with the family since she was sixteen? Well, she's at home with Philippe. We told him we were going to see you but that he couldn't come to see you this time because he had an early start tomorrow. School in the morning, so it was an early night tonight. Marianne was giving him supper when we left and we'll be back in time to read him a bedtime story.'

Chantal gave a nostalgic sigh. 'I always loved the bedtime stories you and I had when we were staying together at your house or mine in Montreuil before Mum and I went to live in Paris, didn't you?'

Julia smiled. 'We lived more like sisters in those days, just like our mothers had been, didn't we?'

Chantal giggled. 'And because our mothers are identical twins I used to wake up sometimes in the night at your house, calling out for my mother. When your mother came in I was convinced she was mine. Oh, hello, Bernard.'

Her cousin-in-law came over and kissed her cheek.

'How are you getting on, Chantal? Are they treating you OK?'

'I'm being spoiled rotten.'

'Even by the exacting Michel?'

Someone else was pushing open the door. Chantal watched as Michel advanced into the crowded side ward. He grinned as he overheard Bernard's comment about him.

Bernard shook his colleague's hand. 'Sorry, Michel, I didn't know you were coming back this evening. Such devotion to duty.'

Michel raised an eyebrow. 'And on my day off too!'

'Actually, we were just leaving. Promised to be back home before Philippe goes to sleep. He adores Marianne but there's nothing like a paternal voice reading the bed-time story, is there?'

Bernard held out his hand to help his wife as she got to her feet.

She smiled up at him. 'Oh, so you're volunteering to read the story tonight, are you?'

'Don't want to tire you out, my love.' He placed a hand gently over Julia's pregnant bump. 'Only a few weeks to go now.'

'Don't forget you promised to make me godmother,' Chantal said.

'You'll be the most perfect godmother,' Julia said as she bent over the bed to give her cousin a kiss.

After they'd gone Michel lost no time in checking out her injured ankle. He looked down at her as his experienced fingers gently palpated the damaged area. She winced but refrained from comment as she looked up at him. His expression was so sensitive, so caring, so totally wrapped up in what his patient had suffered and was going through.

She told herself that was all she was, another patient. And that was how she wanted their relationship to remain.

'Good. The swelling's going down. Sister's done a good job this afternoon.'

He sat down in the chair beside the bed. 'Anything you'd like to ask before I go?'

She found herself wishing she dared ask him to stay longer but instead she shook her head and told him she was sure the nurses would continue to take care of her. Better to dampen down the ridiculous feelings she was experiencing. Who needed male company anyway? Certainly she didn't.

He stood up. 'I'm sure they will. I'll go and see Sister now and find out who's on duty this evening. You must have some supper, Chantal. Got to keep up your strength. I'll be back in the morning to see you.'

She watched as the door closed after him, willing the sad feeling to go away. She knew she mustn't allow these insane seductive feelings about Michel to enter her mind. In her post-Jacques life she'd convinced herself that she could never trust a man with her heart again. She would never open herself up to potential pain. She must remind herself every day and never weaken her resolution.

Michel drove out of the staff car park at a furious rate. He slowed as he started to ascend the narrow winding road to the top of the hill. This was always where he began to relax after he'd been on duty. But today he found it harder than usual to switch off, even though technically, it had been his day off.

Reluctantly he admitted to himself that the problem was Chantal. Ever since she'd joined the staff in Emergency in February he'd been aware of her. She was different from all the others. Someone whose company he enjoyed. But it was a totally platonic feeling. It had been more than three years since Maxine had died and his love for her had grown stronger. Every day he still grieved. But somehow when he was with Chantal he became interested in her as a woman.

Surely, that didn't mean he was being unfaithful to the memory of Maxine, did it? It just meant he was a full-blooded normal male and being with an attractive, intelligent woman like Chantal stirred him. But he wouldn't allow himself to go along with those feelings. Being with her today, touching her skin, smelling the scent of her body had brought it all to a head. He certainly didn't want to act on any of these feelings. Heavens above, she'd been his patient today! He would have to hand her on to a colleague for further treatment.

He got out of the car in his driveway and looked out over the stunning sea view. He turned to watch the sun setting over the hill. He was alone, as he was meant to be for the rest of his life. To love a woman was to risk the bitter pain he'd felt when Maxine had been taken from him. He couldn't risk that again. Not in one lifetime.

CHAPTER TWO

As MICHEL DROVE his car down the hill above St Martin sur Mer he was feeling apprehensive. Even the glorious sea view couldn't distract him from thinking about his work in Emergency today. It had been a month since he'd picked up Chantal from the beach and taken her back to the Hôpital de la Plage. He'd made sure he'd referred her to the orthopaedic ward the day after he'd treated her.

He swallowed hard as he changed into a lower gear. His reasons were obvious only to himself and his colleagues hadn't questioned his decision Basically, they'd followed his advice on the treatment plan he'd recommended and Chantal had been an exemplary patient. Today was the first day she was going to work with him in Emergency for a full day, without the aid of her stick.

He'd been impressed with her absolute determination to cope with the work he'd given her during the last two weeks she'd spent in Emergency on light duties, always aided by her stick and always within reaching distance of a chair in case she became tired.

As he drove through the hospital gates he told himself to stop worrying about her. She was a feisty girl, dependable in any situation. Always cool and unflustered with whatever problems a patient posed. An absolute natural in their department. She'd be able to cope today when he'd scheduled her to work the whole day.

Switching off the engine in the car park, he managed to convince himself that she wasn't his problem. He'd prescribed her treatment and the result was that she had a healthy, viable ankle that shouldn't cause problems in the future. So he should stop thinking about her. There was work to be done and Chantal was just another colleague in his department…wasn't she?

It was ironic that she was the first person he saw as he pushed open the swing doors into Emergency. He couldn't help smiling at her. She looked so young and fresh and raring to go this morning. He had to remember not to treat her any differently from his other colleagues.

'Ready to work all day?'

'Of course! I've dealt with a couple of patients already. No problem.'

She covered the few steps between them, consciously walking correctly, as she'd practised with the physiotherapists; heel toe, heel toe.

'Very good.'

She grinned, unable to stop feeling pleased with herself at his praise.

'Oh, I've had only the best treatment, you know. And I was determined to get back to normal working life as soon as I possibly could.'

'I know you were.' He averted his gaze, which was full of admiration. As his phone rang 'Well, then, let's see what we're landed with today,' he said, getting out his smartphone to scroll through his messages. 'Hold on a moment, Chantal. I may need your help immediately. I'm getting a message through about a car crash on the motorway.'

Even as he spoke the doors to Emergency swung open

and a couple of porters with patients on trolleys followed each other inside. From outside the building came the sound of another ambulance arriving.

'Dr Devine,' the first porter called. 'This woman is in pain and she won't stop screaming. She's completely hysterical. I can't—'

'Let me help you,' Chantal said in a soothingly calm voice as she moved to meet the porter.

'I'll deal with the second patient,' Michel said. 'Contact me whenever you need me.'

Chantal had already directed the porter to take their patient into the nearest vacant cubicle and was leaning over her, trying to reassure her that she was safe. The screams had now turned to sobs as the patient clung to Chantal's hand.

She was aware that Michel had just arrived and was taking his place at the other side of the trolley.

'I've handed my patient to a colleague so I can get the general picture of where I'm needed most. I thought you might need some help here.'

He could see Chantal was having a soothing influence on the hysterical patient as she gently asked her name.

'Josephine,' the patient whispered now in between sobs. 'I will be OK, won't I?'

'Yes, you will. I'm Dr Chantal Winstone and I'm going to do everything I can to help you. Now, tell me where it hurts Josephine. Let me…'

As Chantal began to pull back the blanket covering her patient she was immediately aware of her condition. She was a large lady but it wasn't just due to obesity. She was definitely pregnant.

Chantal held back her own emotions, the feelings she'd had about pregnancy ever since she'd lost her own much-wanted baby sometimes overwhelming. It was only a fleeting memory of the horrors of her miscarriage that came to her. She was a doctor and should be totally dispassionate about any medical situation. When she was needed she had to deal with the case as expertly as possible.

She took a deep breath and for a split second her eyes met Michel's. She mustn't show her conflicting emotions in front of him. The patient always came first.

'Josephine, when is your baby due?' she asked quietly.

'I don't really know with this one, Doctor. This will be my fifth, you see, and I've been so busy I haven't really had time to get to the doctor's. I know I've missed a few periods but I've lost count and... Oh, help me...'

By the time the screaming started again Chantal had removed the blanket and was checking her patient's abdomen. The contraction she could now feel was very strong. A swift examination of the birth canal showed her that the cervix was well dilated.

She glanced up at Michel. 'Call Obstetrics to send a midwife. We can't move our patient up to them at this late stage. And if you could bring me that gas and air apparatus over there by the door?'

Her full attention was back on her patient. 'Breathe deeply, Josephine, deep breaths, breath through the pain. Thanks, Michel.'

She took the mask he'd prepared and fixed it over her patient's face. 'There we go, breathe through now, yes, that's good, very good, keep going like that, Josephine.'

Michel found himself marvelling at how calm Chantal was through all this. No one else in the team who'd rescued their patient from her crashed car on the motorway had suspected she was pregnant. They were working fluidly together now. He'd moved to check on the dilation of the cervix.

'The cervix is fully dilated now, Chantal. I can see the head. Don't let Josephine push until the next contraction. I need to adjust the cord.'

'Pant for the moment, Josephine, breathe short breaths. Excellent. Well done. I'll tell you when you can push. Not yet. OK, now, push, bear down into your bottom, the baby's head has made an appearance. Yes, a little rest for you now…'

She was watching for another signal from Michel. As their eyes met she saw the relief in his, he saw the enigmatic emotions that the baby's delivery had set in motion. Yes, she was deeply involved, not just giving this delivery her all in terms of expertise and experience. She was deeply moved even though outwardly she remained calm and in control.

He wondered if she had an issue with childbirth. Had she had a bad experience somewhere in her own past? Whatever had happened to her, she was a joy to work with now. They dovetailed together as they worked well together.

Josephine was clinging to Chantal's hand.

'You're doing fine, Josephine.'

Michel signalled for a final push. As the baby moved down the birth canal he took it into his hands and it began to cry lustily.

'Here you are, Chantal.'

He was handing her the baby wrapped in a dressing sheet. As she took the baby from him he could see the tears in her eyes, the deep involvement she had with this birth, the tender way she held the precious bundle in her arms. For a moment their eyes met over the baby and Chantal let out a sigh of relief.

'Thank God,' she whispered huskily. 'A live birth is always a miracle.'

For a moment she didn't appear aware of her surroundings. Seconds later she cleared her throat and became totally professional again as very gently she handed the baby to her patient.

'Here's your daughter, Josephine.'

Now it was Josephine's turn to shed tears of joy. 'A daughter! After four boys she's very welcome. I shall call her Chantal, Doctor. You've been so kind to me. I couldn't have got through this without you.'

'Oh, I think you could,' Chantal said, dabbing her eyes with a tissue as she turned away from the joyful scene of mother and baby together.

Suddenly she was aware that Michel was beside her, his hand on her shoulder. 'Are you OK, Chantal?'

'I'm fine.' she said firmly, turning to look up into his eyes. 'It's always an emotional experience when a baby is born, isn't it?'

He was holding onto his own mixed emotions now. He had to get a grip on himself where Chantal was concerned. She disturbed him too much and at this moment he wasn't sure why.

A midwife came into the cubicle. 'I came as soon as I could but— Oh, I see I was too late. Sorry about that but we're very busy in Obstetrics at the moment.'

'Don't worry,' Chantal told her. 'I'll hand Josephine and her daughter over to you now. I haven't done the postnatal checks yet. This is a fifth baby and Josephine was involved in a car crash earlier.'

'I'll leave you to it, Chantal,' Michel said, as he heard her starting on the patient's history with the midwife. 'I'll check on what's happening to the other new patients.

May I suggest you take a break before you work on your next patient?'

She glanced at him enquiringly. What was he implying?

'It's your first day back on full-time duties,' he said, quietly before turning away and leaving the cubicle.

After filling the midwife in with Josephine's details she left her patient and the new baby in her care. Josephine clung to her hand. 'Do you have to leave me, Dr Chantal?'

'I'm afraid so. But you'll be well looked after when you're taken to the postnatal ward.'

She bent down to say goodbye to the baby. The little rosebud mouth was moving as if acknowledging her. She could feel tears prickling behind her eyes as she swiftly became professional again and left the cubicle.

She'd taken Michel's advice and had a short break in the staff coffee bar before she returned to report to him in Emergency. He strode across to meet her as she came in through the swing doors.

'Everything OK? How's the ankle?'

'It's bearing up very well, thank you. You seem to have everything under control here.'

'Yes, we had six patients from the crash. The rest had been allocated to another hospital in this area. Josephine was one of the ones who was totally blameless apparently. So we won't have the police coming in to interview her.'

'Thank goodness for that. Josephine needs rest now to enjoy her new baby.' She heard her voice crack with emotion as she spoke and hoped Michel hadn't noticed.

Michel heard the emotional involvement expressed in Chantal's voice and wondered once more what had happened to her before she'd joined the staff in February.

'So you're fit to work again now, are you?'

'Of course.'

'Well, there's a young boy waiting to be seen in cubicle two. His mother is with him.'

'Fine.' Chantal turned away and went to check on her next patient. She found a small boy who'd just arrived after falling on his way to school. He was crying as he clung to his mother's hand.

'Be quiet, Albert. The doctor's here now.'

Chantal looked down at her patient on the treatment table. He was shivering with shock. She spread a cosy lightweight blanket over him. He stopped shivering and looked up at her enquiringly with wide trusting blue eyes, deciding that this lady doctor was OK. Quite pretty, actually. Nice teeth when she smiled at him, which she was doing now.

Chantal glanced down at the notes that had just been given to her.

'Albert, can you tell me what happened when you were walking to school?'

'There was this dog, you see,' he began tentatively.

Chantal smiled. 'I see. Was it a big dog?'

'Oh, it was enormous! But I'm not scared of dogs, am I, Mum?'

'Not a big boy like you, Albert. Now, tell the nice lady doctor how you ran much too quickly when you chased the dog and tripped up on that kerbstone.'

'So where did you hurt yourself when you fell?'

'All down my leg.' He pulled back the side of the blanket to reveal an improvised bandage of old cloths. 'You should have seen the blood, Doctor.'

'I can see the bloodstains peeping through the bandage, Albert. Who put the bandage on?'

'The lady with the dog. She took me into her house and told me I was a naughty boy for chasing him.'

Chantal could see more tears threatening. 'Mind if I have a look?' She was already peeling off the cloths very carefully so that they wouldn't pull on his skin. 'Oh, yes, now I see the problem. Don't worry, Albert, I'll soon have that sorted.'

'What are you going to do to me? You're not going to chop it off, are you? My friend's dad had to go into hospital to have his leg chopped off. He walks with crutches now. I don't mind having crutches but I'd like to keep my leg on if you don't mind. You see, I play football.'

She gave him a reassuring smile. 'I'm simply going to mend the cut that's appeared in the skin. Can you feel this nice soothing liquid I'm painting all over the cut?'

'What's that for?'

'That's cleaning the wound and—'

'Have I got a wound? Like a soldier?'

'Yes, and you're behaving like a brave little soldier for me. I've just put some painkiller on it so it won't hurt much. Not that you'll need it as you're such a brave boy. How old are you, Albert?'

'Five and a half,' he said proudly.

'You're a big boy for your age.'

Then she fell silent as she focussed on the task in hand. 'There, all done. I've put some stitches in so that—'

'Stitches? How many?'

She solemnly counted them one by one.

'Six.' She was spraying the whole area of affected leg now.

'Six? Wait till I get back to school and show everybody!'

'Doctor, do you think I should keep him at home today?' his mother asked anxiously.

Chantal replied that one day at home would be advisable to give the healing process a good start. She explained how to treat the little boy for the next ten days before his mother took him to see their family doctor who would arrange for the stitches to be taken out.

'Oh, don't they dissolve by themselves?'

'Not this kind of stitches. Because the wound is quite wide and in an area of the leg that will get a lot of movement from an active boy like Albert, it's advisable to put very strong stitches in.'

She pulled back the curtain of her cubicle as she said goodbye to her little patient and his mother. The cubicles were all being used now and further patients were being wheeled in on trolleys.

Better get a move on. Michel didn't like to have too many patients who hadn't been seen by a doctor.

She found herself busy all day with a seemingly endless stream of patients. There was no time to think about herself. She was glad she would be going off duty soon because her ankle was aching now. Actually, it had been aching for the past hour or so but she'd chosen to ignore it. It would be a sign of weakness if she sat down during working hours.

The evening staff were arriving and taking over the patients who were still waiting to be seen. She took the opportunity to go into the office to write her report. Settling herself in front of the computer with her right foot on a chair, she turned sideways and switched on the computer. It was a relief to take the weight off her ankle.

She typed on in her difficult position, listing the wide variety of cases she'd dealt with that day.

Before the crash patients from the motorway had arrived, her first patient had been the child with a frozen pea up his nose. Frozen when it had gone up, according to Dad, but decidedly squelchy and messy when she'd managed to pull it out with her smallest forceps. The blood that came with it was because of the various attempts that had been made to reach it with a variety of household instruments, including a spoon, before the young boy had been brought to Emergency as a last resort.

She'd assured the worried father that the bleeding was only shallow and would stop soon as long as the young patient promised not to pick his delicate little nose.

Following that, there had been the motorbike rider on the coastal road who'd crashed into the back of a car that had stopped suddenly. X-rays had shown a fractured tibia and fibula so she'd called in Orthopaedics to admit him to a ward before they operated on him. The operation had been successful.

'So this is where you're hiding?'

She recognised Michel's voice behind her, lifted her ankle with both hands to support it and turned the desk chair round.

'Don't let me disturb you, Chantal. How does your ankle feel after a whole day on your feet? Tell me honestly. Don't be brave about it.'

'Well, it aches a bit now. It's just because it's tired.'

'OK, that's a warning sign to ease off. Come in after lunch tomorrow and just work the afternoon.'

She raised one eyebrow. 'Are you sure, Michel? I don't want my colleagues to think I'm getting preferential treatment.'

'And why on earth would they think that?'

'Well, I've had a lot of time off recently and…' She felt flustered as she attempted an explanation. 'You're the boss. If you think it's OK then I'd best take your advice.'

He put on a serious expression. 'I'm absolutely certain. Easy does it.'

'You've been so kind to me.' She was merely stating
the obvious while no one was around to hear her prais-
ing him. She just felt she'd had preferential treatment
and had to be careful.

'I'm just being an attentive doctor to a valuable colleague.' His voice was husky. He cleared his throat, before continuing in a totally neutral voice without a hint
of emotion, 'You're a very useful doctor in our department so we don't want to mess up the treatment you've
had at this stage.'

She felt another surge of gratitude. 'I was wondering…'
'Yes?'

'I'm truly grateful for the way you've taken care of
me since I sprained my ankle and I'm sorry for the way
I was so grumpy when you found me lying in the sand.'

'Oh, Chantal, you were suffering from shock. Completely understandable. You were in pain. It was perfectly
natural for you to behave like that. Forget it.'

'Well, I've been thinking.'

She paused as she reflected that she really had been
thinking too much about this delicate situation. It had
started while she'd had to spend a lot of time resting during the early part of her treatment. Now was the time to
act before she lost her nerve.

'I'd like to buy you supper one evening as a means
of thanking you for all your help in getting me back on
my feet'

He was staring at her now, seemingly lost for words.
'Chantal, you don't have to buy me supper.'

'Oh, but I'd like to.'

She'd rehearsed this invitation so often, not knowing
how he would take it. She hadn't meant to deliver it in

this awkward position, sitting sideways to the desk, holding her convalescent ankle with both hands. She must look so ungainly.

'Of course I know you must be busy in the evenings so if—'

'I'd like to take up your offer, Chantal. Thank you. What did you have in mind?'

He was smiling now, trying to lighten up. She'd caught him completely off guard. It had been the last thing he'd expected from her.

'Well, I thought it would be fun to have supper at that old wooden beach café near the place where you rescued me from that killer stone. I used to be taken there for lunch after a morning on the beach at Club Mickey. It was before my father died, I remember.

'Every August my cousin Julia and her brothers came over from England with their parents for a holiday and that was where we'd all meet up. It was such a treat. Our mothers—they're twins—were always there. Our fathers were both English so the conversation over lunch switched from English to French all the time. It was such a happy time in my life.'

He noted the poignant hint of nostalgia in her voice before he spoke to reassure her of his interest in this kind invitation.

'I'd enjoy going to the beach café, Chantal. Actually, I've never got around to visiting it. It looks a quaint sort of place.'

She smiled. 'I'm not surprised you haven't tried it yet. It looks very shabby now. The winter winds and rain mean it needs repainting every summer. They haven't got around to that yet this year but it's got its faithful clientele just the same.'

'Will you make the booking or shall I?'

'Oh, we don't need to book. It's first come first served. Just let me know when you're free.'

'How about tomorrow?'

She hid her surprise at his prompt reply. She'd expected him to defer his answer and then possibly forget about it. She wouldn't have had the nerve to repeat her invitation.

'Yes, that would be good. If I'm only working for the afternoon I won't be tired.'

He nodded. 'That was exactly what I was thinking. We'll go straight there when we come off duty. Now, finish your report as soon as you can and go and rest that ankle on your bed with a pillow to elevate it. Be sure to call Housekeeping and order supper to be brought up to your room.'

'Oh, I didn't know that was possible.'

'All things are possible for the medical staff of the Hôpital de la Plage.'

He was reaching across the desk for the internal phone. 'This is Michel Devine. My colleague Dr Winstone will be resting in her room this evening. Could one of your staff take her a supper tray? Yes, about seven o'clock.'

He broke off to speak to Chantal. 'Coq au vin, omelette, or salade Niçoise?'

'Salade Niçoise, please.'

He relayed the message. 'So I'll see you tomorrow afternoon, Chantal. Now, do rest that ankle.'

He turned and moved towards the door to stop himself regretting his decision to have supper with Chantal. Closing the door after he'd passed through it, he leaned against it, breathing heavily.

'You OK, Dr Devine?'

He hadn't noticed a junior nurse coming along the corridor.

'Yes, I'm fine, thank you, Nurse.' He recovered quickly and smiled down at the young lady who was looking earnestly concerned about him.

He started walking in the other direction. Taking care of Chantal as a colleague posed no problems. But spending a whole evening with her in the romantic setting of the beach as the sun disappeared behind the hills? What was he thinking? It was the sort of situation he'd avoided since Maxine had died. OK he'd play it cool, very cool. No emotional involvement.

Two colleagues having supper together, discussing... well, whatever colleagues are supposed to discuss. Nothing remotely romantic. Books, theatre, cinema. That sort of thing should keep the evening going without too many gaps in the conversation. Ah, she'd lived and worked in Paris, hadn't she? He could leave most of the talking to her.

Chantal could tell it was already morning before she even opened her eyes. She could hear the sound of footsteps hurrying down the corridor. Everybody was going on duty. But she had been ordered to rest.

She opened her eyes and looked at the travel clock on her bedside table. Eight o clock! She hadn't set her alarm for once. No need for that this morning.

The phone rang. It was housekeeping asking if she would like breakfast. Dr Devine had left instructions for them to call. 'Would you like a croissant?'

'Yes, please.'

'And a coffee with milk?'

'Please' She liked dipping her croissant in a large breakfast cup of milky coffee.

She got out of bed and went over to the window, pulling back the curtains. Wall-to-wall sunshine already. Well, it was almost summer. From her window she could see the main gate, the ambulances lined up for duty, one already speeding in from the seafront, making its way to Emergency where everybody would be hard at work by now. Including Michel. She swallowed hard as she thought of her embarrassing attempt to ask him out for supper yesterday evening. She'd been successful but she could tell he had only been polite with her. He would probably be relieved when it was all over. She couldn't think why she'd set it up. Well, actually, she did have an idea but it was too complicated to analyse.

Was she testing herself to see if she really had changed into the ice maiden she tried to portray to the opposite sex? If that was her real reason for this date—if she could even call it that she'd have no problem sticking to the vows she'd made to herself last September. None whatsoever. Her emotions were completely surrounded by ice.

Someone was knocking on her door. She shrugged into her dressing gown and went to open it, taking the breakfast tray from the maid then climbing back into bed.

As she dipped her croissant in the coffee she reflected that her rendezvous with Michel this evening would be harmless as long as she remembered she'd arranged this meal together to thank a kind friend and colleague for all his help. That was the sole object of this evening out together.

'Are you ready to go off duty, Chantal?'

The afternoon had flown by as she'd dealt with an influx of patients from a crash on the coastal road involving a coach and two cars. She was pulling back the curtains from her cubicle as her final patient was being taken away on a trolley to be admitted to Orthopaedics.

'Have all the patients been seen, Michel?'

'Treated, discharged, admitted and no fatalities. The evening staff have all arrived. I've even dealt with the police investigation and sent them on their way satisfied they've got all the medical details they need for their report. Excellent teamwork by everyone this afternoon, so let's go!'

She wasn't fooled by his bright and breezy attitude. He was as apprehensive as she was.

'Give me ten minutes to clean myself up.'

'Ten minutes? You look fine to me. OK. See you by the front entrance.'

She headed for the staff changing room to change into a pair of jeans and tee shirt, adding the white sweater she'd brought to tie around her neck in case it got chilly later on. Not that they were going to stay long enough for the evening chill to set in. A quick supper, a polite chat and they'd go their separate ways, wouldn't they?

She glanced at her reflection. Mmm, not bad. A dash of lipstick and then she would be ready.

Michel was chatting to Sidonie by the main entrance and Chantal slowed her pace. Mustn't seem too eager to be off.

Sidonie broke off the conversation. 'Hi, Chantal. You look like you're off out. Going anywhere nice?'

'Off to the beach café for supper.'

'Oh, that's where you're going Michel, isn't it? Ah, so you're going together? Keeping up the aftercare of your patient? Very commendable. Well, don't let me keep you. Have fun but beware the killer of stones.'

Sidonie smiled at them as she moved away down the corridor.

Chantal was beginning to wish she'd never dreamed

up this supper date. The entire medical staff would have heard about it by tomorrow morning.

'So, shall we go?'

Michel was looking down at her, a wry grin on his face, probably knowing exactly what she was thinking but hoping he was covering up his apprehension better than she was.

CHAPTER THREE

CHANTAL WAS VERY pleased to see that the Café de la Plage was filling up with lots of happy people. She was glad to have got through a busy afternoon working in Emergency and was now ready for some leisure time. She noticed chattering families, a couple of small babies being rocked off to sleep in their pushchairs, one by a serene-looking, white-haired grandmother and the other by a harassed-looking young mother who was also coping with a lively, demanding toddler while Papa was completely engrossed in a dispute with the elder sister.

It was the sort of warm family atmosphere she remembered from when she had been brought in here as a small child by both her parents, before her father had died. She felt safe here, at home, relaxed—well, almost. There was still a nagging doubt at the back of her mind that she could have made a mistake, asking out the boss on the pretext—no, it hadn't been a pretext! It had been a genuine desire to say thank you to a colleague, now a good friend, who'd been extremely helpful in her time of need.

What other possible reason could she have had? After the treatment she'd suffered at the hands of the duplicitous Jacques she didn't trust any man, not even

Michel, who was obviously still in love with his irre-placeable wife.

Michel was holding the back of her chair, politely in-tent on making sure she was comfortable. She hoped they would both relax a bit more when they settled into their table by the window. Their conversation as they had walked across the sand had seemed strained, con-trived almost, as they'd talked about their work and barely glanced at the setting sun, which was low in the sky be-hind the hills, causing a pink blush over the clouds and strands of gold to weave in and out of the lovely scenery.

She'd had the urge to stop and admire it but hadn't known whether Michel had time for such romantic ele-ments in his busy life. His devotion to duty was legend-ary at the hospital. He seemed to live for his work and probably hadn't got time for sunsets and sunrises.

She'd remarked on the sunset a couple of times but Michel had seemed to increase his pace and had appeared to be in a hurry to get the dutiful evening over and done with. Well, that's what it seemed like to her and she was beginning to feel the same way herself now they were inside the café.

She'd arranged this outing so it was her responsibility to make sure it wasn't too painful. She put on her dutiful-hostess smile as she looked across the table at Michel.

'Always a good family atmosphere in here, don't you think?'

'Well, I can't really judge because this is my first time here.'

Chantal decided to try again. 'Of course. As I told you, it's a favourite of mine from childhood.'

'Chantal! My husband didn't tell me you were here!' A plump, rosy-cheeked lady was leaning over the table.

'We haven't had the pleasure of serving you in our restaurant this season. Are you still living in Paris?'

'Ah, Florence. Lovely to see you again. Actually, I've left the Paris hospital. I'm a doctor in Emergency at the Hôpital de la Plage now.'

'A doctor? It's not possible that you're all grown up now. Now, what can I get you and your charming companion?'

Michel extended his hand. 'Michel Devine, *Madame*, a colleague of Chantal's at the hospital.'

Chantal could see that Florence was much impressed by her handsome friend and colleague. He could be really charming when he put on that dazzling smile. Florence was handing out menus now and being extremely deferential to the important-looking doctor.

Decisions were made about what they would choose from the menu. Florence put a bottle of red wine on the table. 'On the house,' she informed them, before returning to her kitchen.

'Cheers. Good health,' Michel said, raising his glass towards Chantal.

They could relax now. Michel was beginning to actually look her in the eyes. He seemed to be studying her face now, as if it was the first time he'd ever really seen her. Well, it was the first time they'd been alone together in an off-duty situation and it felt very strange.

She sipped the wine. Mmm, the house wine was always good here and the first bottle was usually a gift to regular clients.

She looked around her. 'The babies seem to be settling at last.'

Michel smiled. 'I love the sound of families enjoying themselves.' He paused, his voice husky. 'Except it reminds me...'

He was looking down at the table now, tracing the pattern woven into the lace. She waited until he looked across at her a few seconds later. There was a sad expression on his face.

'What does it remind you of?' she prompted gently.

'Oh, it's not important. I was simply going to say…'

'Here you two go, a small starter for you.'

Florence was placing a couple of plates in front of them. There was pâté garnished with a tomato salad and gherkins and a basket containing warm, freshly baked bread in the centre of the table.

Chantal made a mental note to ask Michel what he'd been going to say just now about the families enjoying supper together. It had appeared to have had a profound effect on him. But she wasn't going to pursue that line of conversation at the moment. Not when she was feeling relaxed and could see Michel was enjoying himself at last.

He picked up the bottle and poured more wine into her glass. She knew she would have to slow down on the wine at some point. Still, they weren't driving and if she stumbled on the sand, Michel could always carry her. She suppressed a giggle as she reached for more of the delicious bread to accompany the tasty pâté.

'What's so amusing?'

She laughed. 'I was just reminding myself I've got to walk over the sand near where I sprained my ankle so I'd better go easy on the wine.'

He laughed with her. 'No problem. We coped last time, didn't we?'

'There won't be a repeat tonight, I assure you,' she said firmly, biting into a gherkin.

Florence took away their starter plates and placed a steaming tureen of asparagus soup on the table.

By the time the main course was served Chantal's initial hunger was feeling deliciously appeased. They were both eating the roast-chicken dish much more slowly, talking more across the table, and the wine seemed to be disappearing very quickly. This was definitely a fun evening at last. The ice had been well and truly broken.

They had started discussing the theatres in Paris, shows they'd seen, music that pleased or displeased them. All the worthwhile frills of life that got pushed into the background when they filled their days with work, however important it was.

'Yes, I do find I have to make time for leisure pursuits when I'm living away from Paris,' Chantal said. 'I love the countryside and the sea but sometimes I long to go out to the theatre.'

'There's a very good theatre in Le Touquet. I must take you there one evening.'

'I'd like that.' She would, she really would. Going to the theatre was something that good friends and colleagues could enjoy together without it meaning any commitment on either side.

Florence's husband, Giles, who was now waiting on the tables while Florence concentrated on the cooking, paused beside their table to remove the empty bottle and bring back a new one. Michel was now chatting amicably with Giles about wine. It transpired that Giles's brother had a vineyard near Bordeaux so supplies of good wine were easy to come by.

Chantal could feel herself warming more and more towards Michel. She was seeing sides of his character she'd never seen before. Asking him to come out for supper tonight had been a good idea after all. And whatever her motives might have been, she was enjoying herself, delighted that she was getting to know the real man behind the work-obsessed Michel.

The restaurant was now completely full and people were queuing outside. They'd finished their delicious dessert of raspberry tart when Florence asked if they would like to have their coffee served on the veranda.

Michel said that was an excellent idea. It was one of those splendid early summer evenings that were made to be enjoyed in the fresh air.

Michel chose a secluded table in the corner of the veranda, overlooking the sea. The gentle sound of the waves was so romantic, just the sort of evening for a stroll along the beach, hand in hand with someone close to you. That wouldn't happen with herself and Michel. It was obvious that even though they were enjoying themselves they were both carrying too much baggage from the past.

She took a sip from her coffee cup, her eyes on the man opposite her. His enigmatic expression was giving nothing away. Placing her delicate china cup carefully back on the saucer, she tentatively asked Michel what he'd been going to say when they had first arrived. 'You said this place reminded you of something.'

He tensed. 'Oh, it wasn't important…'

She waited patiently. 'It seemed important to you at the time.'

'Oh, well, it was just a thought about the family atmosphere in the restaurant. I began thinking, as I often do when I'm in a family-orientated place, about what might have been if my wife and I had been able to have children before she died.'

He leaned back in his chair. It had felt as if he was making a confession. Strangely enough it gave him a sense of peace. Chantal was the sort of woman he could trust. She looked as if she would understand what he'd been through, indeed what was an ongoing problem for him, never far from his mind.

Chantal drew in her breath as she looked across the small wicker table, noticing the obvious poignant distress in Michel's expression. A slight breeze from the beach ruffled the edge of the white tablecloth. It was almost as if the ghosts of the past had come to disturb them.

She leaned forward. 'Would you have liked to have had a family?'

He cleared his throat. 'It's my deepest regret that we didn't. It was my wife's cancer that prevented it and then...then she died.'

The silence that ensued was almost palpable. She felt uneasy. Had she caused him more sadness by probing into his past? Maybe if she assured him that she understood something of his pain, that she too had suffered.

'I would have loved to have a baby.' She took another sip of coffee to steady her nerves. Yes, it would help him if she told him what she'd been through and how it had affected her.

She looked out across the sand towards the waves dimly outlined by the lights from the shore. She felt calmness descending on her. Yes, it might help to reassure him that she could understand his distress.

'Last September I was in a long-term relationship with someone. At least, I thought it was permanent. He'd asked me to marry him. He appeared overjoyed when I told him I was pregnant.'

She paused to take a deep breath. 'And then I discovered that he had a wife. I was three months pregnant, looking forward to having our baby. Discovering that Jacques had deceived me triggered a miscarriage.'

Michel reached across the table and took her small hand in his. 'How traumatic for you. The miscarriage that followed his deception…that's impossible to contemplate.'

She nodded, unable to speak for a short while, but the touch of his fingers around hers gave her the strength to continue.

'In the few hours I had between learning the truth and losing the baby I'd already decided that I desperately wanted my baby. I would make every effort to bring up my child in a loving environment. My mother was widowed when I was seven and subsequently she brought me up by herself. She was a wonderful example for me to copy. I planned to give my child the close upbringing that I had with my feisty mother. Even though I would be a single mother I knew I could provide my child with a strong, stable family unit.'

She swallowed hard. 'But that wasn't to be.'

He squeezed her hand. 'Chantal you're young. You've plenty of time to have babies in the future.'

She removed her hand from his grasp and placed it in her lap. It was too upsetting emotionally to have him giving out sympathy when his own suffering was still painful for him.

'Ah, but the problem is I'd have to commit myself and I could never trust my heart to a man again. It would mean opening myself up to potential pain in the future. So I've reconciled myself to the idea that I'm not going to have a family. I've got a good, rewarding career, which totally absorbs me.'

For a few minutes neither of them spoke. They were the only people left outside on the veranda as they looked out at the moonlight shining on the sea. Florence and Giles had retired to their living quarters at the side of the café.

Michel was deep in thought. Such a peaceful scene

would hopefully soothe them both. Dared he broach the subject nearest to his heart?

Gently, he broke the silence. 'I know exactly what you mean. I'm utterly devoted to my work at the hospital. For me, taking care of my patients and staff takes the place of emotional commitment now. I determined after Maxine died that I would never allow the love of a woman to enter my life again. You see, I associate the joy of love with the bitter sensation of loss. I don't allow myself to get close to anyone because of that. My only regret is that it means I'll never have children.'

She nodded. 'Like me, you've had to come to terms with the fact that you'll never have a child. The pain never goes away, does it? Tonight when you saw those happy families you got a sharp reminder of what you will always miss. When I'm in hospital, delivering a baby, holding a little miracle in my arms as I did with our patient from the car crash, when Josephine asked if she could call her baby Chantal...'

She forced herself to continue as he leaned forward, seemingly hanging on her every word. 'When I contemplate a barren future sometimes...'

'But there is a way out.' His voice was devoid of emotion, completely calm as he interrupted her.

She stared at him. 'What do you mean?'

He placed both his hands on the table, palms downward. 'We both want a baby but no commitment to each other,' he said slowly. 'We could be parents of convenience. Don't you think?'

She hesitated before nodding. 'Yes,' she said weakly, her voice a mere whisper as her imagination ran riot. What was Michel getting at? Where was this emotive conversation going?

He stood up, pulling his chair round the table so that

they were closer together. Was he going to suggest something they could do together to realise their dreams? She could smell the scent of his aftershave, his skin, his body so that she could almost feel the testosterone swirling through his powerful manly frame. She was sensually moved by being so close to him. It wasn't possible to discuss something of this nature without being emotionally involved, was it? Should she stop him before he asked her an impossibly intimate question?

He cleared his throat. 'Maybe there's a solution to our problem. We both want the same thing—a baby. Neither of us wants a relationship. We get on well as good friends with no strings attached. It's not beyond the bounds of possibility that we could...'

She held her breath, her emotions churning as she waited for him to explain.

'We must be totally professional about the situation.'

He paused, as if searching for words.

She sat very still, waiting for him to continue. What on earth did he have in mind?

He reached for the glass of brandy that Giles had placed beside his coffee cup before he'd left them alone earlier.

Chantal had studiously ignored hers at first but now she also raised her glass to her lips.

'How would you feel about investigating the possibility of having donor insemination? We would use my sperm to make you pregnant. There are some excellent clinics we could choose from where the procedure could take place.'

She told herself she was relieved that he'd reverted to his medical voice, making it quite clear there was no emotion to be involved in this situation. So why did part of her wish that he wasn't being quite so professional about his suggestion?

'If you did become pregnant I would help you through the pregnancy, giving you support as I did when you sprained your ankle.'

'Michel, pregnancy and caring for a baby is a lot harder than having a sprained ankle!' she told him sharply. 'It's a lifetime's commitment to another human being. We'd have to draw up an agreement about the parenting of our baby, making sure the child was our priority in a completely unselfish way. There would be so many obstacles if we were intent on getting it right, I'm not sure it would work.'

She could see the hope in his eyes disappearing. 'Even though I must admit it's very tempting.'

Even as she said that she told herself she had to be very careful of this man. She mustn't trust any man in a situation where she might find herself depending on him. She must keep her independence at all costs.

'So, what do you think?'

She squared her shoulders. 'You know, in spite of all the problems I can foresee, I do so want to have a baby!'

'That makes two of us!'

He smiled directly into her eyes, that sexy smile that she knew would be one of the obstacles she'd have to deal with. Could she have the baby she longed for without giving in to her natural feelings towards the father of her child?

'Think about it, Chantal. Take your time, no pressure. We've got to agree between us on the parenting involved and so forth. Then we've got to find a discreet clinic where we can be treated and—'

'So many problems to cope with. It's all a bit overwhelming.' The doubts were creeping in already.

'That's why we'll both take our time.' He stood up and

held out his hand to raise her to her feet. 'Let me know if you want to continue with the idea and we'll have another meeting.'

The gentle breeze had turned cold as it blew in from the sea. She shivered.

He pulled off his jacket and put it around her shoulders. 'You're getting cold. We should go. Just don't dismiss my plan completely. It's a pragmatic solution to the problem shared between two good friends. Don't write if off simply because it's not the conventional way of having a baby. Give it some thought.'

As they walked back across the beach he took hold of her hand, telling her to beware of the killer stones that lay beneath the surface of the sand, waiting to pounce onher feet as they had last time they had been here together.

She laughed. That was one of the things she liked about Michel. In spite of the strictly professional image he tried to portray with his staff he was a fun person to spend time with in an off-duty situation. Tonight she'd seen glimpses of the joyous man that he must once have been.

Listening to her laugh, Michel realised he loved the sound of her laughter. He loved lots of things about her. If they did go through with his plan to have a baby together he'd have to be so careful he didn't find himself falling in love with her. Because falling in love was wonderful but the bitter sensation of loss he would feel if or when the love was taken away from him was too awful to contemplate twice in one lifetime.

CHAPTER FOUR

CHANTAL LOOKED AROUND at the patients waiting to be seen in Emergency. The midday sun was streaming through the windows in the waiting room. Summer was well and truly here. Close by on the beach families were enjoying themselves but here in the treatment area the patients were concerned with their pain and anxiety or that of the relative or friend they were accompanying.

She held back the curtain of the cubicle where she'd just treated a patient suffering from sunburn. It could have been worse but she'd advised the mother to keep the child indoors for a few days and then to cover him with hat and loose cotton garments if it was necessary to take him outside.

Applications of non-scented talcum powder would take care of the tiny spots on the chest and underarms which she'd diagnosed as prickly heat. The mother was very young and inexperienced so had hung on every word that Chantal had spoken. She'd also been shown how to rub in the cream she'd been given to soothe the skin where it was particularly painful. The main thing was to avoid direct sunlight and seek shade wherever she could.

Chantal sensed that all eyes were on her now, everybody hoping it was their turn to be seen next. She knew which patient had been waiting for the longest time but her eyes were once again drawn to a young girl seated near the entrance. She must have come in during the time Chantal had been treating the child suffering from sunburn. She looked terribly uncomfortable as she perched on the edge of her seat, pulling a large raincoat around herself. A raincoat, on a day like this?

Chantal walked purposefully across to investigate. 'Is anybody with you, dear?' She kept her tone gentle and encouraging.

The girl pulled the raincoat around her defensively and looked down at the floor to avoid eye contact. How could she explain why she was there when she'd been telling herself she couldn't possibly be pregnant?

For weeks she'd suspected she might be but she'd tried not to think about it. You couldn't get pregnant on the first time, could you? Her fattening tummy and enlarged breasts had convinced her of the awful truth. She'd covered it up for as long as she could but now she knew she needed help. But having got herself to the hospital, she was really scared of what this doctor would say to her.

'Nobody's with me,' she muttered, half to herself.

Chantal made an instant diagnosis that needed to be checked out as soon as possible. This situation couldn't wait. The girl was older than she seemed at first from across the room. Old enough. And a large man's raincoat on a sunny day was a real giveaway.

She took the girl's hand. 'I'd like to help you. Would you like to come along with me?'

She held out her hand. Her patient ignored her hand but began to cry as she made two attempts to stand up. Chantal signalled one of the porters to bring a wheelchair over. They made it into the cubicle before her diagnosis was well and truly confirmed. As the porter lifted the girl onto the treatment couch her waters broke.

Chantal leaned over her patient to remove the sodden raincoat so she could examine her, all the time talking to her soothingly to assure her that she was in good hands. Everyone wanted to help her.

'Would you like to tell me your name?'

'Maria,' was the whispered reply, before the girl's cries became louder. 'No, oh, no, Doctor, Doctor…'

'Don't go,' Chantal told the porter. 'I need you to take us to Obstetrics. Get a trolley, please.'

Seconds later she'd informed Obstetrics she was on her way with a young patient who was in labour.

Maria was clinging to her hand as they made their way through Emergency towards the corridor that led to Obstetrics. She was aware that Michel had spotted her moving out of their department and was striding across to check what was happening. One of the waiting patients had complained to him that he should have been seen next but the lady doctor was taking care of a young girl who'd just arrived.

'I decided this patient needed to jump the queue,' she told him breathlessly, intent on keeping up with the porter and her patient, who was now howling with pain and clinging to Chantal so that she was now bent over the trolley. The porter was holding the door open for her.

She turned her head and paused for a moment to continue her explanation to Michel. 'If you remember when we delivered a baby a few weeks ago in a cubicle it certainly wasn't an ideal situation. Fortunately our baby was OK but…'

'Our baby was more than OK, Chantal, but I take your point. If there's time to get to Obstetrics that will ensure an easier delivery. You certainly seem to have this situation sorted. Keep me informed when you get to Obstetrics.'

As Chantal moved along quickly with her patient she felt disturbed by the way Michel had said 'our baby'. She knew she had to make that life-changing decision soon about whether she and Michel should have their own baby and stop shelving the issue. She brought her whole attention to her patient once more, but at the back of her mind his deep masculine voice was still with her.

'Our baby.'

As Michel went back into Emergency to calm the impatient man he couldn't help thinking that even though Chantal seemed to attract obstetrics patients she still hadn't mentioned the conversation they'd had some time ago on the subject. It had taken all his courage to put the idea to her. After all, it wasn't every day that two colleagues went out for supper and ended up discussing the possibility of having a baby together.

He was relieved, as he glanced around Emergency, to see that one of his colleagues had taken the complaining man into a cubicle and the department was relatively quiet again. He could even hear the constant whirring of the air conditioning.

'Dr Devine, could you help me?' one of his nurses called out.

'Of course. I'm on my way.'

He shelved the problem of Chantal's silence on the subject nearest his heart but not before he'd decided to broach the subject with her as soon as possible. The longer he waited for an answer the harder it would become. Something was nagging him that she'd decided to say no to his unconventional plan, otherwise she would have got back to him in the intervening weeks wouldn't she?

He helped the nurse with her stitching of a wound. She could have done it by herself but seemed to prefer to have him there to supervise the procedure.

The hefty builder lying on the trolley didn't make a sound as the young nurse, her tongue firmly clamped between her teeth, slowly stitched up his wound. The patient looked up at the nurse as she breathed a sigh of relief.

'Didn't feel a thing, Nurse. Tell you what, I bet you were good at embroidery when you were at school last year, weren't you?

'I'm older than you think,' the young nurse said defensively, before glancing up at her boss to see what he'd thought of her prowcss.

'Well done!'

She'd only needed a bit of encouragement. His phone was beeping. He went outside the cubicle.

'Michel, do you mind if I stay with Maria in Obstetrics during the delivery? She's only sixteen and there's nobody with her. The cervix is well dilated so I shouldn't be long.'

'Take as long as you like, Chantal. I'll cover for you and send for extra help.'

He was confident that a quick call to the staffing agency would solve the problem. At this time of year newly qualified doctors had registered with the medical agency he found was the most efficient and were anxious to work in his prestigious Emergency department. He dialled the number.

As he was pressing numbers and waiting to speak to a human voice he reflected that one thing he'd noticed about Chantal was that she bonded with all her patients easily and they loved her for it. She took an interest in each and every one of them. She'd make an excellent mother.

He was still waiting for the agency to get back to him, so he called in his next patient at the same moment he decided to deal with the problem of Chantal this evening when they were both off duty. He couldn't do anything about it while she was fully occupied in the delivery of another baby.

Genevieve, the obstetrics sister, was relieved that Chantal was going to remain with their young patient. She'd been brilliant at calming down the young girl. Sixteen years old and she'd made her own way to the hospital while in the first stage of labour. As naïve a maternity patient as Genevieve had ever met. Nobody had explained the birds and bees to that one!

Chantal leaned over her patient as she showed her how to breathe in the gas and air that helped to take away some of the pain when the contractions came. The poor child…she had to stop thinking about her as a child. Maria had told her she was sixteen. Theoretically adult. Well, adult enough to have conceived a child,though she seemed totally bewildered by what was happening to her now.

From the little information Maria had given her she'd gathered that her mother had died in a road accident when she was small and her father had taken care of her by himself since then but he was often away on business.

Papa worked as a salesman and was in Belgium at the moment. He had a mobile phone but he didn't like Maria phoning him when he was working. Anyway, she'd forgotten the number and she didn't have a mobile herself. Too expensive, her father had told her. He always phoned her on the landline to say when he was coming home. Another contraction was beginning and Maria was concentrating on the breathing Chantal had taught her.

The young girl relaxed her grip on Chantal's hand as the contraction passed.

'You're doing really well, Maria. Is there a relative other than your father that I can call?'

Maria shook her head. 'I'm alone in the house when Dad goes away on business. That's why I came here today. I'd only admitted to myself a few days ago that I was pregnant. I thought I'd better get help so— Ooh, that awful pain's coming again, Chantal, help me.'

'Breathe into the mask, Maria.' She checked with Genevieve, who told her the cervix was almost fully dilated so that their patient could push on the next contraction.

It was a relief when she could tell her patient it was time to bear down. She could push now.

She reached for a dressing sheet and gently mopped Maria's face before the next contraction.

There was a moment of anxiety as she had to tell Maria to stop pushing. Sister was sorting out the cord, which was around the baby's neck.

'Good girl,' Chantal told her patient. 'Yes, one more breath for me, now another. OK, another push and...'

The whole team seemed to exhale a sigh of relief as the baby flopped out into Genevieve's hands. Almost immediately came the wailing cry they all wanted to hear.

As Chantal handed the baby wrapped in a dressing towel into Maria's arms her young patient's eyes were wide with amazement.

'Dr Chantal, I'd put on a bit of weight but I didn't know I was so near to having my baby. I'd tried not to think about it and I daren't tell Papa. Oh, look, it's such a miracle, isn't it? Growing inside me, my baby. I love it. And it's all mine isn't it? Is it a boy or a girl?'

She glanced up at Chantal, who was overwhelmed by

Maria's childlike reaction. 'You've got a little girl, Maria. A beautiful little girl.'

'A girl, I've got a girl! A baby girl!'

Chantal became aware that someone else had joined the team in theatre. She could hear a muted male voice in the background somewhere.

He moved to the foot of the bed. 'I was just checking how things are going up here, Chantal. The staffing agency hasn't replaced you yet but I see you've got your hands full at the moment.'

She smiled across at him. 'This really was a miracle.'

'So I see.'

As their eyes met over the scene she knew she had to go through with their mad plan. She'd been hovering and dithering since that fateful evening at the beach café. And also, in this moment of enlightenment she knew that Michel would be a good, caring man to have a baby with. This rush of sentiment was gratifying but worrying if they were to stick to the original plan Michel had outlined.

'She's a lovely baby,' he said, his voice husky with emotion as he watched Chantal taking the baby from the young mother to start the postnatal checks.

He stayed on for a short time, watching her checking the baby's airway and nasal passages. Now she was gently weighing the precious child watched by the young mother who was totally in awe of her baby and the helpful doctor who'd made it all go so well when she'd been in despair. Chantal seemed totally engrossed in her tasks.

He slipped away unnoticed, even more anxious to find out if she'd given some thought to his plan.

An hour later Chantal had settled the new mother and baby in the postnatal ward, promising to return to see her before she went off duty. She spent a few minutes with Veronique, the mature, sympathetic lady in charge of patient home care, explaining that she was worried about Maria, the young girl in Obstetrics, who'd given birth that morning. She outlined as much as she knew about her patient's difficult background while insisting that further details were required as soon as possible.

Veronique took down the details and promised to go and see Maria that afternoon.

'And please try to get in contact with her father,' Chantal said firmly.

'Don't worry, Dr Winstone. I'll treat Maria's case as a priority.'

Feeling a little more reassured that wheels would turn while she got on with her work in Emergency, Chantal hurried along to report to Michel that she was back. She found him in a cubicle reviving a teenager who'd swum too far out to sea. The lifeguards had brought him into hospital, having spent the few minutes in the ambulance working on him. The seemingly lifeless young man was on his side as one of the lifeguards was working in synchronisation with Michel. Between them they'd just achieved the first signs of life.

Chantal waited as she heard a vague groaning sound from the patient's throat, then more water coming out of his mouth, a flickering of the eyelashes, a valiant attempt to speak followed by a movement of the chest. She watched as Michel continued to work on his patient. She didn't want to disturb him while he and the lifeguards were engrossed in reviving their patient.

Minutes later Michel pulled himself upright and breathed a sigh of relief. 'Thanks for bringing him in, boys.' He smiled at the two young lifeguards. 'We got him just in the nick of time. Another few minutes and it would have been too late.'

He became aware of Chantal standing by the door. 'Good to see you back, Chantal. How are mother and baby?'

Chantal smiled. 'Doing fine in the postnatal ward.'

'That's good! Now, have you had any lunch?'

She shook her head. 'It's too late now. We need to do something about those patients waiting out there. I'd rather keep going till this evening.'

'Me too.' This evening. He mustn't think about the evening yet.

As she went out of the cubicle a nurse was waiting to ask her for help. She'd brought her young patient back from an X-ray of his arm, followed by the plaster room, and she needed a doctor to outline the treatment required. Was he fit to be discharged or should he be admitted? He'd fallen from his bicycle on the promenade and was still in a lot of pain.

Chantal followed the nurse to the treatment room to check on the X-ray of the scaphoid bone, an important wrist bone, and the subsequent application of a rigid plaster. She was glad that the plaster was a temporary one comprising two halves which could be removed or adjusted as necessary. The patient's fingers were very swollen, she noticed.

She phoned Orthopaedics and asked if they could find a bed for a young patient with a fractured scaphoid. She recommended that he be kept in overnight to be seen as soon as possible by a consultant. The plaster needed to be adjusted by an expert and further treatment was necessary.

Then it was on to the next patient in the seemingly endless queue. There was no doubt about it that balmy summer days increased the number of people waiting to be seen in Emergency.

'The evening staff are arriving.' Michel put his head round her cubicle curtain. 'How long will you be?'

She smiled with relief. 'I'm just clearing this trolley.'

'Leave it. That's an order. I'll delegate it to someone who hasn't been working all day like you. Come now, Chantal. I need to ask you something important. My office in two minutes?'

'OK, you're the boss.'

She wondered what the rush was as she followed him after a couple of minutes. She had a feeling it might be because she'd been avoiding him for a while, feeling desperately unsure of the plan he'd asked her to consider.

'That was five minutes.' He stood up from behind his desk as she went in.

'Yes, it was.' She sank down into the chair near his desk. 'Where's the fire?'

He grinned. 'You can slow down now I've got you here.'

He sat down again and some of the bravado he'd exuded disappeared. All he had to do was say he needed an answer. Yes or no to his master plan? Looking across at Chantal, he realised he'd suddenly run out of steam. She looked as tired as he felt. Maybe it wasn't a good idea to ask her to dinner this evening after all. They'd both been working flat out all day and he expected a lucid answer to his all-important question. Yes or no, not maybe, or give me some more time.

He cleared his throat. It was now or never; take the bull by the horns.

'I've been wondering if you'd had any thoughts on what we discussed at the beach café that evening?'

'Oh, yes, I've given it some thought and…Michel, are you OK?' She was concerned by the agitated way he was now pacing the floor, not looking directly at her and breathing really deeply.

'I'm fine!' he snapped. 'So what conclusion have you come to?

She stood up and walked over to the window where he was now leaning against the wooden shutters fixed back to reveal the evening sun.

'I've given it a great deal of thought.'

'You have? And?'

'I made enquiries at a discreet little clinic I know of in Paris. I spoke over the phone with the director and explained our situation. He assured me they would be able to set the wheels in motion as soon as we come in for an appointment. If, after a consultation and the necessary tests, we wish to proceed, they would be pleased to help us.'

'And would you be happy to go ahead, Chantal?'

She could see the beads of sweat on his brow as he continued speaking. She had to put him out of his misery.

'Yes, I would,' she said, with a confidence that belied the worries still haunting her about the whole project.

He let out a sigh of relief. 'So that's the first hurdle over. You'd taken so long to get back to me I'd given up hope.'

'Michel, this isn't something to be entered into lightly. I've spent many hours agonising over the problems we could face if we go ahead.'

'Me too. That's why I think we need a proper meeting. I've drawn up a list of shared parenting requirements I'd like to discuss with you. Would you care to have supper with me this evening at my house? That way we won't be disturbed by waiters or nearby diners overhearing our unconventional conversation.'

She hesitated. 'Are you sure you feel like making supper this evening?'

Strike while the iron is hot! 'It won't be anything brilliant. An omelette or something simple. We've both skipped lunch so a cardboard box would taste good.'

She laughed and the tense atmosphere began to evaporate.

'Now, this is something I've got to see. A man who can make a meal out of a cardboard box.'

CHAPTER FIVE

THEY CALLED IN at the small store that had been turned into a supermarket since the time when she had come here as a child. This had been in the days when her father had still been alive and they had often came over from nearby Montreuil for a day on the beach. Later, when she and her mother had moved to Paris and had been staying in the area during the long summer vacation she would come in here with other members of her family.

She had particularly enjoyed coming in with cousin Julia, clutching the spending money her mother had given her and deciding whether to blow it all on sweets, a drink or an ice cream. Situated at the end of the promenade, it had been the perfect place for children who had been lucky enough to have some money or an indulgent grown-up with them. In those days, she remembered, it had been a grocery store with a very good bakery attached.

This evening they needed provisions for their supper. Michel had told her he knew there were eggs at home but he was a bit vague about anything else. They definitely needed fresh bread.

'I've never done much shopping,' Michel told her, his expression conveying that he found the whole experience boring.

He was following her, looking a bit lost as they walked down the first aisle. 'As I told you, Chantal, I can whisk up a decent omelette; possibly add something like cheese or ham.'

He reached forward and took packets of both as if anxious to get out of this unfamiliar place as quickly as possible.

Chantal could see that he rarely did any shopping. 'I'll get some salad and bread, Michel. I can see the baguettes over there.'

'I'll get some wine and meet you in the next aisle.'

As she got some freshly baked bread she could see Michel discussing wine over the other side of the shop. He may dislike shopping for food but he seemed to understand his wines. He called her over and she hurried across.

The man serving in the wine area was holding out a glass of wine for her to taste. 'Your husband suggested you taste this one and this one.'

Michel hadn't flinched or corrected the mistake as he watched her putting the glass to her lips, swirling the wine in the glass to let it breathe, as her mother had taught her when she'd been old enough to have a small glass with lunch or supper.

'I prefer this one,' she said, as she made her choice. She had found it difficult to decide. They were both fine wines.

Michel smiled. 'Good choice.' Both men nodded sagely.

As she moved on she heard Michel arranging for a case of wine to be put in his car.

He joined her shortly afterwards, now looking very pleased with himself. A more relaxed Michel was emerg-

ing from the work-weary man who could barely disguise
his dislike of mundane matters like shopping.

At last they were now into the idea of eating and the
trolley began to fill up with impulse buys. They were
both feeling hungry so it was soon brimming over. Chantal remembered neither of them had eaten any lunch. Michel was nowhere to be seen now.

She found him at the dessert counter, where he was
pointing to a large apple tart and asking the serving lady
to wrap it for them. 'I'll take some of that cream and some
crème fraîche to go with it.'

As they made their way out of the shop, Chantal found
they were both in a more relaxed mood. The tension between them as they had entered had been almost palpable.
They'd worked all day and had been starving but they'd
had to face the dreaded shopping before getting home
and cooking. But she'd found it fun to turn what might
have been a chore into a pleasant experience.

'We've got far too much food,' she said, as they piled
the goodies into the boot of Michel's car.

He smiled. 'As my grandmother used to say, *'Appetite
comes when you eat.'*

Chantal laughed. 'Absolutely true! But you'll find
yourself eating for days to come with this amount of
fresh food, though some of it will freeze, of course.'

He opened the passenger door for her. She climbed in
and fastened her seat belt. As they began driving up the
hill she looked out at the sun low in the sky at the top of
the hill. Below on the sea twilight was dancing on the
gentle waves, a golden glow telling them that the day was
over and the pleasures of the evening were before them.

Yes, they had a serious subject to discuss but they both
wanted the same outcome, a baby to satisfy their crav-
ing for parenthood. Parenthood without commitment to

each other. She turned sideways to look at Michel. He was looking relaxed, happy even. It could work, this unconventional plan of his. It would work if they were both one hundred per cent committed to the plan.

They were reaching the top of the hill. She could now see a magnificent house standing by itself in a prime position in terms of its view. That couldn't be Michel's house, could it? She held her breath as he turned off the road and swung into the gravel drive.

He turned off the engine and for a few seconds they both remained still, taking in the magnificent view of the sea below them.

'Wow!' she breathed. 'What a view.'

'The view is the reason I bought this place. I'd inherited some money from my grandparents, who brought me up after my parents died. My grandfather was a successful businessman and he had no other relatives to leave his money to. I was an only child. When I got my job at the Hôpital de la Plage I felt I needed a place I could call home, a place where I could put down roots. It was meant to take my mind off the fact that I was on my own now. My consolations were my absorbing work at the hospital and my beautiful house to come home to. Come and look inside.'

A master switch by the door flicked on the lighting system as they went into the spacious hall. There were table lamps, hidden lights in alcoves to light up the pictures on all the walls. Obviously, Michel enjoyed his art collection.

He also enjoyed his photographs. On the hall table there were two photographs of Michel and his wife. One showed them enjoying themselves on a beach, palm trees in the background, his arm around her slender waist. They were both in swimwear, white shorts for him, white

bikini for her. The second was their wedding photo taken
as they'd stood on the steps of the church. They were a
good-looking bride and groom. She could almost feel the
love between them.

She experienced a weird sensation of disturbing emotions, which she couldn't understand. She told herself she
was happy that Michel had known real love and sad that
it had all ended for him. Yes, that was why she felt so
upset, why she didn't trust herself to speak as she turned
away and focussed her attention on a picture of the view
from the house.

She could feel the warmth of the day lingering in the
closed-in atmosphere. He went to open a window as she
followed him into the spacious kitchen. She glanced
around her. It was an absolutely ideal kitchen. The space
would be a pure joy to work in for someone who had time
to cook for a family or throw large dinner parties but
Michel didn't exactly fit into that category.

The kitchen resembled something out of an expensive,
glossy magazine but it didn't look lived in. Some of the
appliances had obviously never been used.

'What's this for?' She put her hand on an expensive-
looking piece of equipment that had been integrated along
a wall of electric appliances.

He grinned boyishly. 'I've no idea! I only know how to
work the important stuff like the cooker. And occasionally the washing machine when I've forgotten to put out
my stuff for the woman who comes in from the agency
once a week to keep the place clean.'

He pressed a switch and quiet classical music started.

'Rachmaninov,' she said. 'One of my favourite com-
posers.'

He nodded. 'Me too. You know, the man I bought
this house from was in charge of a firm that supplied

houses fully furnished to order. His client had defaulted so I bought the house because I liked the view. As long as I've got a cooker, a fridge, music at the flick of a switch and a bed, that's all I'm interested in.'

'It's absolutely wonderful but…'

'Go on, though I know what you're going to say.'

'Do you?' She hoped not. If she was honest she would tell him that it lacked a woman's touch. It lacked any feeling that it was a home.

'You were going to tell me it's like a bachelor pad, weren't you? A place where a man can lay this head at the end of the day.'

She gave him a wry smile. 'You said that, not me.'

'I said it because it's true. It serves its purpose.'

He was uncorking a bottle of wine as he spoke. 'Let's take our drinks on the terrace. That's my favourite place.'

'I can see why.' She settled herself among the cushions on the long wicker sofa as he handed her a glass then sat down at the other end. There were small tables at each end but only one looked as if it had been used. The other still had a label prominently displayed.

'You're quite right, Michel, it's the view that makes this place.'

'And the people in it.' He smiled. 'Thank you for agreeing to have out meeting up here.' He cleared his throat. 'It will be easier to discuss the problems we might encounter with our parenting plan if we haven't got anyone else overhearing us. You say you've already contacted a clinic in Paris?'

She took a sip of wine as she warmed to her subject. 'The director of the clinic is a former colleague of mine. He and his wife became personal friends. They used to give excellent dinner parties. He's an obstetrician/ gynaecologist who took early retirement so that he could open his own clinic to help couples who want a baby but need some kind of conception assistance. Most of his work is with fertility problems but he's agreed to check out our plan for donor insemination.'

'Sounds good so far. I've been drawing up a list of parenting responsibilities which we must take very seriously.'

He broke off to move closer to her on the sofa, bringing the bottle with him so he could top up her glass.

At first she felt as if she should be taking notes, but somewhere along the way they were distracted by talking about their backgrounds. She started it by asking Michel how old he'd been when his parents had died.

'I think it's important to know things that our child will need to know,' she explained. 'Conventional, normal couples will already know these things.'

'Oh, absolutely!' He took a deep breath. 'I suppose the rest of the world will regard us as abnormal but if we can ignore the gossip, that will be half the battle. With regard to my background, both my parents were only children.'

He paused and cleared his throat. 'I was also an only child. I was three years old when my parents died. They'd left me with my grandparents when they'd gone off to the Alps for their annual skiing holiday. They were both swept away in an avalanche.'

'What a dreadful thing to happen. And you were only three.'

He nodded. 'I became aware that my parents had been away from home for longer than usual and started to ask questions about when they were coming back. It's difficult for a three-year-old to understand what an accident is. I missed them, but gradually I stopped asking questions and simply accepted that my grandparents had taken their place.'

She could hear that his voice was full of sadness. A sudden image of him as a lonely child flashed into her mind and she felt sorry for him. And now as an adult he still had no family of his own. She was glad she was going to help him. Yes, that was why sometimes she couldn't understand her own emotions when she was with him. It was nothing to do with the fact that he was handsome, charming and charismatic. None of that came into the equation.

She glanced across at him and saw that there was still an air of sadness which had lingered since he told her about losing his parents.

Michel stood up and escaped into the kitchen as if he didn't want to be seen displaying his emotions.

When he returned he was carrying more nibbles. Cheese straws this time.

She saw the dampness on his cheek as he went past her and once more she felt sorry for the poor little orphan he'd been and was glad that he'd had grandparents to care for him.

'And you?' he enquired, when he was settled once more beside her. 'I remember you said your mother had brought you up by herself.'

'Yes. My father died of cancer. There was a tumour in his oesophagus that was too far advanced to be removed. He was there at my seventh birthday party. I remember wondering why he didn't eat any of the birthday cake my mother had made. A few weeks later he died.'

He put his hand on hers. Neither of them spoke.

'Maybe this is why we're both so committed to becoming parents,' he said gently. 'We both feel we've missed out in some way. To have two parents must be a wonderful experience when you're growing up.'

'We'll have to make sure we give our baby a lot of

loving care.' She looked at the man sitting beside her. He would make a wonderful father.

'Come on, let's carry on this conversation in the kitchen,' he said, holding out his hand to help her to her feet.

She felt it was a very special moment as they stood together, looking into each other's eyes. She held her breath as he leaned forward to kiss her on the lips. As quickly as their lips met the kiss ended. Both of them knew this wasn't part of the contract. It was as if they were agreeing to the start of their journey together.

His arm was resting lightly on her waist as he took her into the kitchen

'So, which of these many packages would you like me to unpack?'

They both surveyed the kitchen table. 'I really fancy watching you whip up an omelette,' she said. 'I'll make a salad and that's the main course sorted.'

'And all this?'

'You've got an enormous fridge-freezer over there, which we'll put to good use.' She was already rinsing the salad ingredients, then mixed a French dressing.

'Got any mustard?'

'No idea. If I have, it will be in that cupboard.'

She found some and added it to her dressing.

'I'm amazed!' she told him as she watched him cracking eggs into a bowl. 'You look like a real chef.'

He laughed. 'Don't be deceived. This is the only dish I can make. You can serve it up at any point in the day, breakfast, lunch, supper. Now all I've got to do is to whisk it like this then into the pan I prepared earlier and, hey, presto! Oh, I forgot the ham.'

Chantal added it quickly. As she helped him turn out the omelette onto a large serving plate they both stood back to admire their handiwork. Michel might be a wizard in the operating theatre but his pride in a simple omelette was a joy to behold.

He sat at the head of the long kitchen table. She sat beside him. They tore off pieces of bread from the baguette, dunking it in Chantal's vinaigrette, drinking the delicious wine, chattering all the time as if they'd known each other for a long time.

'I'll phone for a taxi to take you back to hospital later, Chantal. This wine was a really good choice. I mustn't drive now. Alternatively, I've got a guest room where you could spend the night. No need for you to decide yet.'

Michel found himself working out exactly how long he'd known this wonderful woman. It had been February when she'd first come into his life so she'd been here about four months now. She'd made such a difference to his working life in Emergency. He found he looked forward to working with her every day. And now she was bringing hope into his life by agreeing to have his baby. Their baby.

If he hadn't decided that he daren't love again it would be very easy to feel emotional about her. But to fall in love was not part of the plan. He couldn't open up his heart to the love of a woman again. Chantal, being very level-headed, had her own reasons not to fall in love. She couldn't trust a man ever again. So they were perfect together, weren't they?

He put down his fork and reached for her small hand. 'You won't change your mind, will you, Chantal?' he asked huskily.

She felt the warmth of his hand around hers and the touch of skin against skin seemed almost erotic. She could feel deep down that being with Michel was affecting her more than it should.

'No, of course I won't change my mind.' She stood up. 'Dessert?' she asked briskly.

He could feel something like an electric current running between them. Deep down inside him was a powerful feeling of wanting to take Chantal in his arms and hold her until the feeling went away. He stood up and put his arms around her, drawing her close. This didn't make sense. She should have pushed him away, told him to stick to the plan. Maybe she was feeling as he was. He bent his head to kiss her.

She parted her lips as every sense in her body ignited with passion and longing. She was feeling overwhelmed by the sensual fluidity of her body as she moulded herself against Michel's hard, virile, muscular frame. She was melting away as he held her tightly in his arms. There was a powerful force gripping her. She knew she should fight it but she had no intention of doing so. She didn't even want to stir in his arms in case the dream ended.

He lifted her into his arms, carrying her towards the door. There was no need for words as he carried her upstairs. They were both intent on giving in to the magic of the moment. There was no need to justify his actions or her compliance. Life was too precious to banish moments like this. There was no yesterday, no tomorrow, simply the present moment.

CHAPTER SIX

WHAT HAD HE DONE? How could he have suspended all rational thinking last night? Michel settled himself back against his pillow. He'd lain for a while with his eyes closed. He could hear the steady breathing beside him. With his eyes now open he dared to look at the sleeping Chantal beside him.

He held his breath in wonder. If he were a real romantic—which he'd tried so hard not to be since he'd lost Maxine—he would say she was a vision of loveliness. Her long dark hair, free from the chignon she swirled it into during working hours, was spread over the pillow. Her lips, slightly parted, were impossibly appealing. He remembered the taste of them from last night. The wickedly sensual effect they'd had on him. How could he have given in to that irresistible desire to make love to Chantal?

He'd done so much damage last night. This was an item that definitely hadn't been on the agenda. They'd agreed to be parents of convenience, not lovers.

He swallowed hard as her lovely long eyelashes fluttered open.

'Hi.'

She gave him a shy but sexy smile before looking around her uncertainly. And then it all came rushing back to her. As wonderful as her memories were of last night, it certainly hadn't been supposed to happen.

She struggled to pull herself into a sitting position but he put out his hand to hold her still, trying not to touch the naked skin beneath the rumpled sheets, that same naked skin he'd explored, tasted, kissed. It had been the most wonderful experience. So unexpected. Now what?

'I'll get some coffee, Chantal.'

He was trying hard to blot out the memory of the magic of their night together. His body had so craved the physical side of a relationship that he'd seemed to have forgotten he shouldn't make love to Chantal. She was out of bounds if they were to have a successful agreement of non-commitment.

He ran a hand through his ruffled hair as he sat on the edge of the bed, his back to Chantal. He daren't turn to look at her. Even now his treacherous body seemed hell bent on leading him into danger again. He had to pull himself together and see if he could bring them back on course. Giving in would change everything in the kind of relationship they'd agreed on.

He grabbed his robe from the floor and stood up purposefully.

She lay very still as she saw him shrugging into his towelling robe. This was the most bizarre situation she'd ever been in. Two people arranging to make a baby together in an unconventional and unromantic way had spent the night together and changed the very nature of the relationship they'd agreed to. Emotional feelings had got the better of them last night and they'd been carried away on a tide of passion and desire for each other. They'd ignored the original plan. So what would happen now?

She looked around the palatial bedroom. Swathes of ivory silk curtains were still drawn back from the windows in their ornamental tiebacks. They'd slept all night with the windows uncovered and a couple of windows wide open. She remembered at one point how he'd insisted they go out onto the balcony to admire the moon. So he was a romantic after all. He'd kept that hidden before but not last night!

The garden had been so silent and still, fragrant with the scent of the roses. Michel had insisted he could smell the salty sea but she'd said they were too high up. She'd laughed as they'd argued until he'd kissed her so long and hard that they'd had to move back to bed to resume their lovemaking.

Yes, at the time it had felt like love. But love for each other wasn't on the cards. They'd both said that they would love their baby but loving each other was off limits if they were to keep their independence. They'd both agreed not to commit to each other. They must keep their independence if their original plan was to work.

She climbed out of bed and went into the en suite bathroom. There was a spare bathrobe hanging on a hook. Very masculine, much too large. She was glad it wasn't a feminine type of guest robe. Even as the thought entered her head she told herself that although they hoped to be parents together they shouldn't be jealous of future partnerships either of them might make.

She pulled on the enormous robe and tied the belt twice around her waist as she heard Michel had come back into the bedroom.

She found him on the balcony, placing a tray with croissants and coffee on the small table. She sank down into the large armchair, noticing that he'd replaced the cushions that had been inside the bedroom when they'd both shared the one chair, leaning against each other for warmth, comfort and… She could feel herself blushing at the thought of what had happened next.

'How do you take your coffee, Chantal?'

'Black, no sugar. Oh, you've brought croissants. Breakfast, no less. I'd like milk with my coffee so I can dip my croissant in it.'

He gave her a nervous smile as he passed her cup. 'Strange, having breakfast together.'

'Yes.' It was even stranger, in retrospect, remembering their night together.

They remained silent as they looked out across the garden.

Chantal broke the silence. 'It's even more beautiful in day light out here.'

He couldn't help thinking she looked even more beautiful in the sunshine. That was a wicked thought, a remnant of last night lingering too long. He brought his mind back on track again.

'So, how do we approach the situation now?'

'You mean making a baby together?' She wished she'd phrased that more delicately.

He took a deep breath. 'Well, we both seem well qualified in the baby-making department but…' he paused as if to choose his words carefully '…that wasn't what we intended, was it? We intended to keep our independence and arrange to be parents of convenience. As I see it, we should try to forget last night ever happened and continue with our original plan. What do you think, Chantal?'

'I agree with you absolutely.'

Her treacherous heart was telling her otherwise but

she knew she could never trust another man so she banished all her lingering romantic feelings. She'd learned her lesson the hard way with the deceitful Jacques. Last night had been wonderful but it mustn't be repeated if they were to avoid complications.

'Yes, Michel, our original plan for non-commitment to each other will be the most workable solution to becoming parents.'

Michel nodded his assent. He'd enjoyed every moment they'd spent with each other but he'd got his errant feelings under control once more. He mustn't commit himself to Chantal. He'd never stopped loving Maxine and never could. Even if he could banish his memories of her, he'd promised himself never to risk loving a woman again. If he continued to nurture Chantal in a loving way how would he cope if he lost her? Life could be so unpredictable. Grief was a terrible emotion.

'I think we should stick to our original plan,' he said quietly. 'We must try to forget last night. I'm sorry, I shouldn't have…'

She could see he was worried now. 'Michel, it was a one-off experience. Let's stick to our plan as we outlined last night before we…before we both got carried away.'

'Yes, nothing has changed, has it?'

'Nothing has changed,' she repeated quietly as she thought what a false statement that was. False but necessary if they were to envisage shared parenthood and retain their independence from each other.

To make her point, she held out her hand towards him. 'Let's shake on that.'

He stood up and came round the back of her chair to take her hand in his and draw her to her feet. Deliberately she straightened her arm so that they could now shake hands. It was time go back into the sane world where life would go on as usual.

It was business as usual as soon as they got back into hospital. There had been another RTA on the road that fed the traffic into the dual carriageway and patients were being diverted to all hospitals within a reasonable distance. They'd been chosen to take their share of the injured.

By a tremendous effort of mind Chantal managed to put herself into work mode and behave normally when she was working alongside Michel. When he asked her to assist him in the treatment of a difficult leg injury soon after they arrived in Emergency she was totally professional and relieved with the way that he too seemed oblivious to all that had passed between them only hours ago.

'I'd hoped Orthopaedics would take this young man to Theatre but all the theatres are in use at the moment and this operation can't wait.'

Michel looked over the top of his mask at the small emergency team he'd assembled in the larger of the two treatment rooms.

'Scalpel, Chantal.'

He made a long incision down the side of the injured leg. 'As you can see, everybody,' he continued in his teaching voice, 'the tibia, which as you all know is the strongest and most important bone in the lower leg, has been shattered into several small pieces. You will remember I showed you the damaged leg on the X-rays.'

He broke off to speak to his anaesthetist about the condition of their patient. Reassured by his reply, he continued.

'I'm now going to wire the shards of bone together. I always think it's a bit like doing a jigsaw puzzle when

I have to deal with a large bone as badly shattered as this one.'

Chantal glanced up at the video screen recording the operation above the table. She could see Michel's hands skilfully fixing the tibia together. He too was taking a look at the screen now as he worked on a difficult section. Their eyes met and she could tell he was smiling beneath his mask. She smiled back, a smile that was meant to reassure him that nothing in their plan had changed. If she continued to make every effort to convince herself it would all work out as they'd planned.

As she was moving between patients later that morning she was surprised at a request from the obstetrics department. Could she spare a few minutes to go and see a returning patient who'd asked to see her? She glanced around the waiting area. Five minutes would be OK, she told the person who'd phoned. There were no urgent cases at the moment.

'It's Maria who wants to see you, Chantal. You remember the young woman who came in by herself and was already in labour?'

'Yes, of course. I'm on my way.

Maria was looking radiantly happy when Chantal arrived in Outpatients. So different from the bedraggled girl in the enormous raincoat who'd been well into labour without knowing what was happening.

'I just wanted to thank you for helping me when my baby was born, Doctor. I'd like to call her Chantal. I hope you don't mind if I give her your name.'

Chantal smiled. 'Of course I don't mind! I'm delighted.'

She wondered how many more babies she delivered would be called Chantal. There was a woman with Maria proudly holding the baby who was wearing a pink frilly frock and a tiny hat with a brim that flopped over her forehead.

'I'm baby Chantal's grandmother,' the woman explained.

'A very young grandmother, may I say.'

'Well, my son, the father of this dear little baby, is only eighteen. I was only eighteen when he was born so you can work out how old I am. It was a surprise to me when the hospital contacted me to say Maria had given them my number to call because her father was on business and couldn't be contacted.'

Maria spoke up, looking a little bit flustered. 'Frederick and I had gone out together a few times even though we'd only…well, you know…done it once and I thought you couldn't get pregnant the first time.'

Chantal glanced at the young grandmother. 'Maria isn't the only young girl to believe that old story, is she?'

The grandmother smiled. 'It happens all the time. Anyway, fortunately I can give her all the help she needs. Maria and the baby have moved in with us. Frederick is thrilled to bits at being a father. I've got three more children at home so it's nice to have a baby in the family as well.'

'So you and Maria's father are happy with the arrangement?'

There was a slight pause. 'Let's say he's relieved his daughter is being well looked after, Doctor. He's not really a family man, if you know what I mean. Without his wife he reverted to being a bachelor again and I think Maria was—'

'I was in the way,' Maria said quietly. 'I love being part of Frederick's family.'

'Thank you for coming along to see us, Doctor. Maria

told me all about you. She's just been back for a check-up and everything's fine. You did a great job that day.'

'Thank you.'

Chantal felt a warm glow of happiness inside her as she walked back along the corridor to Emergency.

'You're looking pleased with yourself.'

They'd almost bumped into each other as they'd both hurried around the same corner going in opposite directions.

Her warm glow seemed to get warmer now, especially in her face. How stupid of her to start blushing like a teenager again.

'Michel! Where are you heading off to?'

'As your boss I should be asking you where you've been,' he said in a pseudo-stern voice.

'Got a request to go and see an ex-patient who was having a check-up in Obstetrics outpatients. Do you remember that young girl, Maria, who was in labour when she arrived and I took her to Obstetrics?'

'And ended up spending hours delivering her baby while I was left doing your work and mine.'

He was continuing to tease her with his big-boss manner, while trying to convince himself that nothing had changed between them since yesterday. Yes, he certainly did remember that particular delivery room where he'd been strangely moved as he'd looked at Chantal holding the newborn baby. He remembered thinking what a wonderful mother she would make.

'I didn't spend hours. It was a quick delivery for a first timer. Anyway she's doing well. The baby's eighteen-year-old father is delighted that his mother has accepted Maria and baby Chantal into their large family.'

'They'll all grow up together. One big happy family. Got to go. I'm needed in orthopaedics. They've got a vacant operating theatre at last but no surgeon. Thanks for your assistance in our converted treatment room, Chantal. You did well under the circumstances.'

As he hurried away he knew he would have praised his assistant more if it had been anyone else. But he had to be careful now that he'd shown her how much she meant to him. He mustn't get carried away again, must he? He wasn't at all sure about that. It was going to take an enormous amount of self-control.

She finished writing her end-of-the-day report and switched off her computer. They'd gradually treated all the patients from the RTA and the normal influx of patients. It had been a long day. A long day following a long night. She would have an early night tonight.

'I thought I might find you here.'

Chantal looked up enquiringly as Michel walked in. 'Did you want to see me?'

He perched on the edge of the desk. 'I've been invited to a medical conference in Paris, which starts tomorrow. I had it pencilled in to go over and give a paper there on one of the days, but they've just contacted me to ask if I can be there from tomorrow and stay for the whole of the conference.'

'One of the perks of the job,' she observed dryly. 'How long will you be in Paris?'

'A couple of weeks, possibly longer. Actually, we'll be working hard all the time.'

'Of course you will. And who will be in charge of the department while you're away?'

'The staffing agency is attempting to find a consultant to replace me.'

She stood up. 'I'm sure we'll cope without you.'

'I'm sure you will.'

In a way a break from constantly seeing Michel on a day-to-day basis was what she needed. She would find it hard and would miss him terribly. But at the back of her mind there was a problem that had been niggling her all day. She'd only admitted it to herself when she'd taken a short coffee break in the middle of the afternoon.

They'd made love last night using no protection. She knew the rhythms of her own body as she'd tested the most fertile period in her menstrual cycle before she'd got pregnant with Jacques.

And last night she'd been at her most fertile. If she'd conceived a child naturally, how would that affect their plan? If she'd conceived during their romantic lovemaking then their whole relationship would change, wouldn't it?

'Are you all right, Chantal?'

He was coming round the desk. She forced herself to stand so that she could escape while she was thinking rationally. If he came any closer, if he bent his head near to her as he was doing now...

'I've had a long day, that's all.'

She turned her cheek towards him so that they could say goodbye in the typically French way of a chaste kiss on both sides of the face.

'I've got to go,' she told him breathlessly as the touch of his lips disturbed her more than she'd anticipated.

'Goodnight, Chantal,' he said quietly as he reached the door before she did. He held it open for her. 'Have a good evening.'

'And you, Michel. I hope all goes well at the conference.'

He leaned against the door after she'd gone, taking deep breaths to calm himself. He was glad they'd been sensible just now. Even lightly touching her skin with his

lips had disturbed him. Yes, he was going to need more
self-control to ensure the original plan was going to work.
It was just as well they were going to be separated for a
couple of weeks. By the time he got back he would have
completely forgotten their night of heavenly madness.

CHAPTER SEVEN

AS SHE LAY in her lonely single bed in the medics quarters her thoughts turned to the wonderful night of passion she'd spent with Michel a few days ago. She remembered how they'd had to work together the next day. She'd forced herself to give all her attention and expertise to the patients she had treated. Then in the evening as she had been preparing to go off duty he had told her he had to be in Paris the next day for a conference.

In a way she felt relieved that they would have space between them for a couple of weeks. The brief discussion they'd had when they'd had breakfast together on the morning after their impromptu night of lovemaking had reinforced the idea that they should stick to their original plan. No commitment to each other, parents of convenience. It was easy to say but she was going to find it difficult to implement.

Even now, after just a few days of Michel's absence in Paris, she found herself looking forward to his return. She realised that however she tried to think otherwise, the events of that evening had affected everything they'd planned.

They'd both agreed they wanted to keep their independence, their single status. They would make a baby together, be the most caring parents it was possible to be, given the unconventional circumstances and also the busy professional and domestic lives they would lead. But having thrown caution to the wind and spent the night together, it was difficult for her to forget.

She got out of bed and went over to the window. It was already after midnight but sleep was a long time coming tonight. Dim lights showed in all the wards. She could make out one of the operating theatres, lights blazing as an emergency operation was taking place. An ambulance was pulling up by the entrance to Emergency. One of the night porters and a nurse were already waiting. The hospital never slept, a bit like her at the moment.

She climbed back into bed, leaving the window wide open. There was no air-conditioning in her room. Even a single cotton sheet made her feel too warm. She wondered if Michel was sleeping peacefully in Paris or was he awake, worrying about their relationship? Maybe he was enjoying the bright lights of Paris. There was no reason why he shouldn't. There was no place in her life for jealousy, she told herself firmly. They had no commitment to each other.

She sighed as the sound of an ambulance outside the hospital brought her back to the real world again. The last few days hadn't been easy, especially when she felt as if she was in limbo with the possibility that she might be pregnant already.

They'd only meant to discuss creating a baby by donor insemination. They hadn't meant to go the natural, romantic, intimate way. That usually meant committing to each other far more than they'd meant to do if they were to retain their independence.

She turned over in her bed as she considered the implications. If, in fact, she was pregnant already, that could have a significant effect on their future relationship.

Sleep came eventually but in the morning she had to admit that she was finding these restless nights were depleting her strength. Maybe when her period came she could relax again.

If it comes, said the small nagging voice in her head.

She made sure she was totally professional and efficient during the time Michel was in Paris. The replacement director was good at his job, very helpful and easy to work with. She didn't have time to worry about her personal life as the days passed very quickly. It was only at night she found herself worrying about her relationship with Michel.

She told herself there was nothing she could do about it until he came back from Paris, which would be within the next few days. Michel had phoned to say he and a few of his colleagues were extending their time in Paris for professional reasons. And why not?

The day her period was due came. No period. Not surprising, considering the way she was worrying. She told herself to relax. Two weeks had passed since she'd spent the night with Michel. She would nip out during her lunch-break and pick up a pregnancy kit at the pharmacy.

That evening she shut herself in her small bathroom.

She stared at the thin blue line. Positive. It could be a mistake, but it was unlikely. Modern pregnancy tests were almost one hundred per cent accurate. She had a gut feeling that it was correct. If they'd been planning natural conception on that fateful night, they couldn't have made more effort.

Her initial reaction was that she should phone Michel on his mobile. She reached for hers as she pulled on her slippers then stopped herself from making the call. He would be back from Paris soon. It would be better to tell

him face to face. He could be having a night out to celebrate the end of the conference. He wouldn't want her
babbling something over the phone about…

Her ring tone was playing. She checked. It was Michel.

She took a deep breath. 'Michel, you must be tele-
pathic. I was just going to call you.'

'Anything in particular?'

It was so good to hear his voice again. 'Just checking
when you're coming back. We need to talk.'

'Well, that's why I'm calling. I'm still working tomorrow morning with a couple of colleagues, tying up loose
ends, speaking to the press—that sort of thing. I wondered if you could come over on the train so we could
visit your clinic? Do you think you could make an appointment?'

'I could try.'

Her mind was jumping around all over the place. It
would be reassuring for her to see her friend and former
colleague Sebastian, the director of the clinic. He was an
obstetrician/gynaecologist who would give them good advice about the dilemma they'd brought upon themselves.
She felt so confused. Maybe it was her pregnancy hormones kicking in but she couldn't think straight. Half of
her was completely thrilled about her pregnancy while
the other half, the sensible half, was worrying about all
the implications.

'Will your boss give you a couple of days off?'

'A couple of days?'

'Well, you'll need to stay the night and we can travel
back together the next morning. In fact, if you can't get
an appointment at the clinic tomorrow afternoon, try
for the following morning. OK? I've got to go, Chantal.'

She could hear voices in the background and music
as he gave her details of where they should meet. She

wasn't jealous of him enjoying an evening in Paris, was she? Jealousy where their relationship was concerned must be ruled out at all costs.

She cut the connection and phoned the clinic in Paris.

Paris was always exciting when she arrived after being away for a while. As she stepped off the train and made her way through the crowds the indescribable hub of sound enveloped her. The sights and sounds and even the smell of Paris were unique. She still thought of it as coming home. Her little apartment in the sixteenth arrondissement would be empty.

While she'd been on the train she'd phoned her mother, who was taking an extended vacation near Bordeaux, to tell her she was going to Paris for a couple of days and would call in to see her and probably stay the night. Did her mother want her to send on her mail? Not necessary. Apparently the concierge was already sending everything for her.

The good thing about her mother was that she didn't ask probing questions. Never had. She just let her daughter get on with her life. As soon as she'd gone into her teens she'd felt independent—until Jacques had come along. And now there was Michel. Totally different situations to deal with. She shouldn't compare them.

She hurried down the steps of the Metro. The intense warmth and stuffiness of the Metro got worse the lower she went. It was great in winter but overwhelming on a hot summer day like this. Jumping on the train as the doors were about to close, she felt the welcome rush of air-conditioning. That was better.

She'd always liked jumping on to the Metro and setting off on a journey. Her mother had allowed her to travel by herself from her early teens, having coached her about possible dangers from an early age when they'd travelled together.

It had always been exciting to be travelling by herself. Another step in her independence had been when, soon after she'd qualified as a doctor, her mother had bought the apartment next to her own and given it to Chantal.

It seemed to her that after the years of financial struggle her mother had experienced she loved to take care of her only child. She'd been a teacher all her life but now in her retirement, with a decent pension and a chunk of savings, she could afford to be generous. Chantal felt truly blessed to have such a mother.

As the train drew to a halt at Ranelagh station she was still thinking about what a success her mother had made of her life. Bringing up a child as a single mother had been tough. Chantal was glad her mother could now afford to take long holidays like the one she was enjoying at the moment in Arcachon on the coast near Bordeaux.

She emerged from the stuffy depths of the Metro and turned along the Avenue Mozart. She knew the sixteenth arrondissement from her childhood. Her mother had taught at the Lycée Molière and so they'd based themselves in an apartment nearby.

She had no problem finding the name of the hotel Michel had given her. She gave his name to the concierge, who handed the internal phone to her when he'd established contact.

Michel arrived in the lobby shortly after they'd spoken. She could feel the nervous tension between them as they exchanged chaste kisses on the cheek, like distant friends meeting after a long period of time.

'Have you had lunch?'

'A snack on the train.'

'Do we have an appointment at the clinic?'

She nodded. 'Three o'clock.' She handed him the address. 'It's not far. Would you like to walk and get some fresh air? It's a lovely day out there and I've been cooped up on trains all morning.'

She was beginning to feel quite faint. She took a deep breath.

He put a hand on the back of her waist as they went out into the street. 'Are you OK?'

'I'm fine.'

He took hold of her hand as they walked together. She began to feel stronger. She decided she wouldn't tell him about the pregnancy test while they were walking. They had plenty of time before their appointment. There would be time to find an opportunity before they went in to see Sebastian.

After several streets with high-rise apartments that blocked out the sunshine they came to the edge of the Bois de Boulogne. The sun filtered through the leaves of the majestic trees towering above them as they skirted along the roadside path.

She pointed out the clinic in the distance. The closer they got the more it began to look like a private house.

'That's exactly what it is. Sebastian and his wife Susanne have lived there all their married life. They brought up four children there and now there's often a sprinkling of grandchildren playing in the garden.'

Michel looked around him as they were ushered into a comfortable waiting room. It didn't seem like a clinic. A welcoming sort of place. He smiled his approval at Chantal.

'I'm glad you chose somewhere far away from our hospital,' he whispered as they sank down into a couple of squashy armchairs.

'Absolutely,' she whispered back. There was another couple across the other side of the room within earshot. She hoped they would go in soon so that she could tell Michel her news. The burden of her secret was beginning to make her nervous. The sooner they could discuss the implications, the better.

The door to the consulting room opened and Sebastian came out, smiling broadly as he extended his hand towards them. 'Chantal, so good to see you.'

As she introduced Michel she saw a second consulting-room door open and the other couple were being ushered in. Of course Sebastian would employ other doctors to work with him nowadays. Too late to break her news to Michel now.

'So fill me in about what you've been up to since we last met.'

She leaned forward in the armchair and looked across at Sebastian. As succinctly as possible she explained that she and Michel were good friends and colleagues who, having lost their partners, regretted the fact that they weren't parents and had decided to explore the possibility of having a baby together through donor insemination.

'So you want to obviate the normal course of having a sexual relationship and a commitment to each other?'

'Exactly!' Michel leaned forward now they'd got that out of the way. 'I will be the sperm donor and Chantal will carry the baby. We do have our reasons.'

Sebastian smiled reassuringly. 'I don't need to know your reasons unless you want to discuss them with me.'

He waited to give them a few moments to consider his words.

Chantal knew this was where she had to intervene. The fact that she was already pregnant was overwhelming her.

'There's something I have to tell you before we go any further, Sebastian. It's a very recent development but extremely relevant.'

She was desperately aware that both men were staring at her now.

Michel's face was a total enigma. As he looked at her fumbling uneasily with her words he suddenly had a blinding flash of intuition. He knew the truth.

He swallowed hard as she managed to speak again.

'I'm already pregnant!'

It was so good to be walking along the leafy footpath again. They'd spoken very little to each other since her announcement. At first Sebastian had been overjoyed at what she told him, saying that solved their problem didn't it?

Both she and Michel had affirmed that they would have to rethink their relationship. Somewhat bewildered, Sebastian had suggested they go away and come back to see him in when Chantal was about three months pregnant. By that time he could scan Chantal's abdomen and everything would be clearer, relationships, prenatal care and so forth. He'd had only one question to ask regarding the conception. Was Michel the father of this child?

As Chantal sat down on a wooden bench with a view of the Lac Superieur, the larger of the two lakes in the Bois de Boulogne, she could see a man sweating hard as he rowed past. His sweetheart, lover, wife, whatever, was fanning herself with a magazine in the back of the boat. Romance was everywhere in the summer.

'Well, I'm sure we've given Sebastian something to think about today.'

She smiled as she remembered the learned obstetrician's face as he'd tried to conduct a rational discussion with them.

She turned to look at Michel. 'Sebastian is a family man. He couldn't see why we were being so clinical about the process of conception. To him the best way to get pregnant is the natural way. He has to help too many couples who can't conceive naturally. He can't think why we're not totally delighted.'

Michel was staring at her now, thinking that if only they could both get rid of the emotional baggage from their past lives their relationship would be so much easier.

'Let's go back to the hotel,' he said gently, holding out his hand towards her. 'We need to talk.'

CHAPTER EIGHT

THEY WALKED SLOWLY back along the leafy path that gave them shade from the hot sun before turning into the road leading in the direction of the hotel. There was no need for conversation. Both of them were lost in their own thoughts. Michel was holding her hand firmly as if he was afraid she might fall on the rough causeway. It was a new experience for him to have an unborn child in his care that wasn't a patient of his. A baby that he'd created, with the help of this beautiful woman beside him.

It had been an out of this world experience that he was trying hard to forget now. He knew the original plan was the best course of action. He must keep reminding himself that fatherhood was all he wanted.

Chantal was also thinking about the wonder of being pregnant again. She'd known the joy of carrying her first unborn child but that had lasted only three months. She was remembering how she'd had a completely different outlook on life, a feeling of responsibility to another human being. That was coming back to her now. Especially since Sebastian had confirmed her pregnancy. Michel had been over the moon when she'd emerged from the examination room.

He tightened his grip on her hand as they began to cross the road. She turned her head and smiled up at him.

'I know what you're going through,' she said gently as they crossed to the other side.

'Do you? I doubt it.' He gave her a wry smile. 'I've just learned that I'm going to be a father and the responsibility is overwhelming.'

'That's what I mean. I felt exactly the same with my first pregnancy. But that was short-lived and a totally different situation from this. I thought I had a partner who would stand by me. I was wrong. But there are definitely two of us committed to being good parents to our child this time, right?'

He fell silent again as the possibility of losing Chantal in childbirth taunted him. That was rare in countries where medical care was advanced, but it should never be discounted. He realised his strong feelings for Chantal were intensifying the more he was with her. That was only natural when she was going to be the mother of his baby.

She stood still at the top of one of the side roads. 'I'd like to take a slight detour to show you my apartment.'

'That would be interesting. Is it let to someone else at the moment?

They were already walking down the Rue de l'Assomption. 'No. My mother bought two apartments next to each other when I passed my final medical exams and I became financially independent for the first time in my life.'

'It looks as if it's a pricey sort of area around here.'

'It is, but we were very lucky. My mother had been paying rent for several years on one of the apartments. She scrimped and saved to pay the rent, telling me that it was important she bring up her daughter in a good neighbourhood. She became head of department in the prestigious *lycée* where she was teaching and the salary increase helped enormously. I was also a pupil there so it was a perfect arrangement for a mother bringing up her daughter by herself.'

'Your mother sounds like a remarkable woman.'

'Oh, she is! That's why I knew I could do the same if I had a child by myself.'

His grip on her hand tightened. 'But you won't be by yourself. I'll be there as part of the parenting partnership. Always remember we're in this together, Chantal.'

'Yes, of course we are.'

As she stood in front of the tall, prestigious building where she lived, she felt a moment of panic at the enormity of agreeing to have a baby with someone who would be committed to the baby but not to her. There were so many possible pitfalls along the way.

As she looked up towards her apartment on the fourth floor she had a sudden longing to hide away up there until she knew exactly what it would be like to go through with this unpredictable, unconventional plan. Her apartment could be her bolthole if things got too difficult. She could always return there if ever she felt overwhelmed by future circumstances.

The concierge had come to the door to check on the couple looking up at the apartments. He walked down the steps as soon as he recognised Chantal and they chatted for a short time. She told him her mother was enjoying her holiday. As for herself, she was happy at the hospital she was working in on the coast near Le Touquet. No, she didn't have time to call in because she and her colleague were in a hurry.

Walking off down the street, she knew the concierge had probably found her totally unlike her usual chatty self. But she didn't want to inadvertently divulge any information about her new situation until she'd come to terms with it herself. As the months progressed her secret would be obvious to everyone.

'I've got the apartment right next door to my mother's,' she told Michel, who was no longer holding her hand, sensing her desire to remain discreet in her own neighbourhood.

'You're very lucky to have such an arrangement in a neighbourhood like this.'

They turned the corner and walked more quickly along the Avenue Mozart back to their hotel. He took the keys to two rooms from the concierge at Reception. They went up in the lift.

'You've got the room next door to mine. I was wondering if you'd like to go out this evening for supper.'

She hesitated. 'To be honest, I'm feeling tired.' she said. 'I need a long soak in the bath before I make any plans.'

He smiled down at her. 'Come and have a drink in my room when you feel rested. Take your time. I'll order something from room service if you like.'

She went into her room and headed straight to her bathroom. Good, there was an enormous bath. Large fluffy towels. A nice long soak and she'd be a new woman.

Half an hour later she was in jeans and tee shirt, packed at the last minute in case she found herself in a casual situation during this flying visit. As she knocked on Michel's door she realised she was now feeling so relaxed after her long soak that her feet were still bare. And she was wearing no make-up.

'Goodness, Chantal. I don't think I've ever seen you looking so casual.'

'That's because we're staying in tonight.' As she walked into his room she could smell that indefinable aroma of his aftershave. A decidedly sexy aroma she'd decided the last time he'd worn it. The night their baby had been conceived.

He looked into the small fridge. 'What non-alcoholic drink would you like, Dr Winstone?'

'OK, Dr Devine, I get the message. You don't approve of alcohol for pregnant women, so you're in luck. Neither do I. Not a drop shall pass my lips until I deliver our baby. Is that an orange juice I can spy in there?'

'Yes, and it says it's freshly squeezed, although I doubt it. Anyway, it's the healthiest drink I can find.'

He carried the glass across to a small table by the window, plumping up the cushion in the armchair, waiting to check she was comfortably ensconced before he collected his own drink from the fridge. She felt a frisson of happiness running through her as she watched him.

They were both committed to the child she was carrying. But at this precise moment she found herself hoping Michel would play a big part in her life as well as the baby's. The baby was growing inside her and Michel was growing on her. She told herself that her hormones were affecting the way she thought about the father of her child. These feelings she had for him were only natural. But she mustn't get carried away. She had to stick to the plan they'd agreed on.

For one thing, Michel still loved Maxine. It was obvious to everyone who knew him at the hospital. He'd buried his heart with his wife. He didn't want to move on. If she wanted their relationship to become a real one she couldn't compete with a ghost.

The whole idea was that they should be good parents whilst retaining their independence. She'd had a real relationship with Jacques, who'd gone back to his wife. She knew this arrangement with Michel was ideal. She could have a child and still keep her independence.

She'd got over the spell of nostalgia that had struck her as she'd looked up at her apartment. Yes, it could be her bolthole if it became necessary but for tonight she'd settle for the two of them chilling out in their slippers or, in her case, barefoot.

Michel said it would be a good idea to have an early supper. Better for the baby and also he was planning they should catch an early train so they could be at the hospital by midday. She suggested something light for supper and they settled on chicken and salad. While they were waiting Michel called to reserve their train seats for the morning.

Chantal surveyed the well-presented supper when it arrived. The waiter was at pains to set it all out on a small table, spreading a crisp white cloth and placing a large napkin on her lap. She almost wished she'd made the effort to dress up.

'I feel my old jeans don't match the occasion,' she said when the waiter had disappeared.

'You'd look good in a sack.'

She laughed. 'I didn't have a sack so I pulled on the next best thing.'

She blinked as she found herself falling asleep in the chair. The waiter had already cleared away and she was feeling decidedly sleepy.

She stirred in her chair. 'Time for me to go back to my room.'

'Do you have to? I mean go back to your room? I've got two beds in my bedroom both with clean sheets on.'

He held out his hands to help her stand up. 'I'm so sleepy I don't mind where I sleep.'

He was standing at the door of his bedroom, holding out his hands invitingly now.

'Come and have a look.'

He moved to take her hands as she stood up.

She looked into the bedroom. 'This room does look more inviting than mine.'

He smiled. 'Which bed would you like?'

'I'll have this one.'

'If you open that drawer they've even provided a night-dress for the lady guest and pyjamas for the man.'

'This hotel has certainly been upgraded since my schoolfriends and I walked past.'

She realised she was waking up now, talking quickly, feeling embarrassed that she'd practically invited herself into his bedroom. As she hurried into the bathroom she remembered how she'd told herself she mustn't sleep with him tonight. She'd drunk only orange juice and bottled water this evening so it had been a conscious decision? She couldn't justify it in any way except her own desire to be near him tonight. Blame it on her hormones again. She didn't want to be alone if she could be near her baby's father. Perfectly natural a mother-to-be should feel that way.

Having justified her desires to herself, she unwrapped the new toothbrush from its packet and scrubbed vigorously. Raising her eyes to the mirror, she saw her intense expression and decided to calm down. She'd made a baby with Michel. There was no need to be shy. She knew she hated sleeping by herself in a hotel. That was the only reason she'd wanted to stay with Michel, wasn't it?

She was in her bed when he came out of the bathroom. He came across and sat on the edge of her bed.

They both started to speak at the same time and then burst out laughing.

'You first,' Michel said.

'I was only going to say that I don't think we should…'

'So was I.'

'What?'

He drew in his breath. 'From a medical point of view I think you need to rest and get a good night's sleep after your exhausting day.'

She smiled. 'Exactly. I just didn't want to sleep alone tonight so…'

'Neither did I. Move over.'

She hesitated. He looked so sexy in his robe, his hair, still wet from the shower, was flopping over his face. She wanted his arms around her, to reassure her that all would be well. But if he put his arms around her…

Too late. She felt him draw her against his naked body.

'Do you have to wear this scratchy, lacy thing?' He was fumbling with the buttons.

She helped him. 'But we mustn't.'

'Absolutely not! But a goodnight kiss won't harm the baby.'

It was the longest, sexiest, most languorous kiss she could ever imagine. She wanted it to go on for ever. She wanted it to develop into something more, despite her earlier vow that they must never complicate things further by making love again.

It was a good thing that Michel had more will-power than she did.

With a large sigh, he dragged himself away. 'Goodnight, Chantal.'

'Don't go,' she whispered. 'Just stay there. Hold me in your arms, nothing more.'

Michel took her in his arms again. He'd always thought

of her as being strong, resilient, independent woman. But he sensed that being pregnant again, being in an unconventional situation and all the other problems she was having to deal with, had made her feel vulnerable, unsure of herself.

'I'll always be here when you need me,' he whispered, as she curled herself against him. It was taking all his will-power not to make love to her. He remembered the way she'd clung to him when he'd been inside her on the night they'd made their baby. It was all he could do not to throw caution to the winds and but he had to stay strong.

Someone was tapping on the door. Michel shrugged into the robe he'd dropped on the floor beside the bed when he'd climbed in with Chantal.

He took the tray from the waiter at the door. Placing it on the bedside table he was pleased to see that the waiter had brought coffee and croissants, enough for two people. Chantal could smell coffee, hear someone pouring it. She opened her eyes then pulled herself up against the pillows so that she could accept the cup and saucer he was holding out for her.

He thought once again how young she looked without make-up. And without that tough exterior she tried to portray. That independence she insisted on. But he'd held her in his arms all night and sensed how vulnerable she really was, scared even. At one point she'd seemed to be having a nightmare. He'd cradled her like a baby, shushed her back to sleeping peacefully. She hadn't woken.

He mustn't start falling for her. She was proud of her independence. Wouldn't surrender it to anyone. He must respect that. It was part of her tough personality. The personality that made her so endearing. He mustn't become emotional about her just because she was carrying their baby.

Rather brusquely he asked her if she would like a croissant to dip in her coffee in that disgustingly messy way.

She grinned. 'You remembered! Of course I do. Especially if someone else is going to sort out my bed after I've gone. What time is the train?'

He told her. 'So we'll have to get a move on.'

She swallowed a piece of croissant which had just the right amount of coffee soaked into it. 'Michel, thank you for taking care of me last night. I don't like sleeping alone in a hotel. I felt very safe and I slept like a log.'

'Of course you did,' he told her, wishing she didn't look so beautiful this morning. He'd have to be a robot not to want to take her in his arms again.

He stood up. 'I'll go and use the bathroom.'

'You can have it all to yourself. Throw me a robe and I'll disappear next door.'

The train was about to depart. Michel raced down the platform, having told Chantal to walk slowly.

He was holding out his hand to help her up the step. 'Take your time.'

She was glad they were travelling in first class. So much more comfortable. Michel took out his laptop and became immersed in writing up notes from the conference. Even though she'd slept all night she still felt tired. Good for the baby, she told herself as she closed her eyes.

As they headed for work Michel told her to take her lunch break before reporting for duty. He was carrying her small overnight bag. 'I'll have this taken up to your room. But have lunch first before you go up for a nap.'

'Michel, I slept on the train.'

'Well, have a lie-down, then. I don't want to see you on duty before two o clock and that's an order.'

As she watched him disappearing into Emergency she found herself wishing he wouldn't use that phrase! At times it amused her. She knew he only said it for a bit of fun but she hated it when he turned back into her ultra-efficient boss. She wanted the real Michel back again. She needed that warm, comforting, sexy man. The man she was trying not to fall in love with.

Because if that happened her life would change for ever and she didn't want that to happen, did she?

CHAPTER NINE

DURING THE WEEKS that followed her obstetric appointment in Paris with Sebastian she found herself looking forward to the next appointment when she would see the scan, the technological proof that she was indeed carrying a baby. She'd seen many scans during her professional life but the excitement of seeing that image on screen would be mind-blowing for her. And also for Michel, who'd insisted he wouldn't miss it for anything. It was in his diary and he'd rescheduled his professional commitments where necessary.

As she waited for her patient to return from X-Ray she couldn't help wishing that Michel would be a bit more relaxed about her prenatal care. She tried to remind herself that when he fussed over her—because that was what it felt like to be told she had to take a break or she must eat lunch—she knew he was worrying about the child she was carrying. His child was all-important to him. She was merely the vessel that was carrying the baby. Well, that's what they'd agreed, wasn't it?

But she realised she'd broken the rules when she'd spent the night at the hotel in Paris. But the care and affection he'd shown her was his way of caring for their unborn child. She had to keep reminding herself it was their child that was important to him and not allow his concern for her welfare to overwhelm her.

Or maybe she should have a word with him. He probably didn't realise how much it was getting on her nerves. Or perhaps she should blame it on her hormones, which made her oversensitive?

The opportunity to speak about it came sooner than she'd anticipated.

A young nurse looked into her cubicle. 'Dr Winstone, we've got a child in the next cubicle with spots all over his back. Would you have a look at him for me?'

The curtain was closed again and she distinctly heard Michel speaking to the nurse in his professional director voice. She waited, not wanting to interfere.

Seconds later he came into the cubicle. 'Chantal. I've told nurse to ask someone else to check the child's spots. Obviously, in your condition you mustn't treat any case that might be infectious.'

'Michel, you've got to stop trying to wrap me in cotton wool!'

She hadn't meant to lose her temper but now he really knew how she felt. 'Our colleagues are beginning to talk about us. They're asking questions about our relationship. Take that heavy man with the hernia you stopped me from treating in case I tried to move him onto his side. I know you took over and treated him yourself but that's not the point!'

'So what is the point you're trying to make?' he asked patiently. He told himself he had to make allowances for her condition. Pregnant women were prone to being oversensitive. He would listen and try to calm her down. 'It's not good for the baby if you upset yourself like this.'

She took a deep breath. He'd made it quite plain that everything was for the good of the baby. He wasn't thinking about her as a person. That shouldn't annoy her, given the terms of their agreement, but it did.

She lowered her voice. 'The point I'm trying to make, Michel, is that everybody will soon know we're having a baby together. We can't keep it a secret. Our baby will grow bigger and bigger and then it will arrive, and at that point…'

'Don't patronise me. I understand the situation better than you do.'

A porter was pushing his way through the curtains with her X-rayed patient.

'See me in my office this evening before you go off duty, Dr Winstone,' Michel said in a pseudo-stern tone as he left the cubicle.

The porter was looking perturbed by their exchange. 'On the carpet tonight, are you, Chantal?'

'Possibly,' she said in her most professional voice as she took the X-rays from the nurse who'd accompanied her patient.

The patient raised his head. 'So is my ankle broken, Doctor?'

She placed a cushion under the man's head as she slotted the X-rays into the scanner on the wall. Pointing to the injured area, she showed him the shattered calcaneum, which had been badly crushed as he'd fallen from a tree in his garden and had taken his full weight on one leg.

She could see it would require expert pinning under general anaesthetic or with an epidural before the foot was put in a cast.

'I'm going to ask one of the orthopaedic consultants to have a look at you. If you don't mind waiting here a bit longer, Guillaume, I'll have you seen as soon as I can.'

Guillaume grinned. 'I'm not going anywhere, doctor. The branches on that tree will have to wait until I get out of here.'

Chantal smiled at him. He was a plucky man, hadn't complained at all even though it had been obvious he'd been in pain when he'd arrived.

'Take my advice and get a professional tree surgeon in.'

'That's what my wife said last week. Wish I'd listened to her.'

'Where's your wife now?'

'Funnily enough, she's on duty here in hospital. She's a nurse on the children's ward and hates to be disturbed when she's on duty. Thinks it's unprofessional if I phone her mobile, which is usually switched off anyway.'

'Guillaume, you've got to let her know. With your permission I'll contact the ward now and have her come down here.'

'OK, got to face the music some time, I suppose.' He rolled his eyes. 'She'll be so mad at me. I would have been fine if that ladder hadn't twisted.'

Chantal was already speaking to the sister in charge of the children's ward.

'There, your wife is on her way, Guillaume, and I know you'll find her very sympathetic. I've also arranged for a consultant to be with you as soon as he's finished operating.'

Another nurse had just hurried into the cubicle.

'Darling, I don't believe it!'

Guillaume's very concerned but flustered wife had arrived and was bending over her husband. 'Are you OK? Oh, you shouldn't have gone up that old ladder. I told you—'

She broke off in mid-flow and turned to Chantal. 'Is my husband OK, Doctor?'

'He's fractured his calcaneum so I've referred him to one of our orthopaedic consultants who'll be here shortly.'

'Are those his X-rays?'

'Yes.'

'He's going to need surgery, isn't he?'

'I would think so but that's up to the consultant to decide.'

'Of course.'

The distraught wife lavished attention on her husband, who seemed relieved that he wasn't being reprimanded any more. In fact, Chantal could see he was positively enjoying his wife's concern for him.

She waited until the consultant had arrived, assessed the patient and arranged to have him admitted to Orthopaedics for pre-op care.

Sitting at the computer at the end of her working day, she was typing in Guillaume's details, having just made a call to Orthopaedics. The latest news from the ward was that her patient had had the ankle pinned under epidural and was sitting up in bed, enjoying the lavish attentions of his wife.

She heard the door opening and half turned to see who it was.

'Ah, I believe you wanted to see me this evening, Dr Devine.' She swung round from the computer to give him her full attention.

'Chantal, you did realise I was joking this morning when you were treating Guillaume, didn't you?'

'Of course I did. But you had the porter worried. He asked me if I was on the carpet this evening.'

He smiled. 'Have you anything more to report?'

She hesitated. She needed to clear the air, speak about their altercation while he was in a good mood. 'Michel,

I've got serious issues with the way you've been treating me since I became pregnant. I don't mind you making fun of me but fussing about my delicate condition is definitely off limits.'

'Not when you're carrying my child,' he said, quietly.

'Our child!'

He sat down on the edge of the desk. 'You really are annoyed with me, aren't you? Look, it's to be expected in the early days of pregnancy. Your hormones—'

'There you go again.' She lowered her voice. 'There's nothing wrong with my hormones.'

She stood up, folding her arms defensively in front of herself.

He strode across the room and drew her gently into his arms. For a few moments she resisted him, standing rigidly, arms like a shield in front of her. But one glance up at his amused expression broke her resolve.

'Maybe I am being a bit over-sensitive,' she conceded quietly.

He bent his head and kissed her, gently, persuasively, ready to agree to any terms she wanted to set if only he could make her happy again.

As he considered the enormity of what she was doing, carrying this baby for him, he found it impossible not to hold her more closely and tenderly against him. He was hoping she wouldn't interpret his tenderness as being too possessive. He released her from his arms just in case he'd got it wrong again.

'So remind me, what's the date of the scan? I know it's in my diary. Next week, isn't it?'

'Next Wednesday.'

'We'll have to make it a day trip. I've got an important meeting on Thursday. Could you get the scan around two in the afternoon?'

'I've already booked one-thirty.'

'Excellent. And, Chantal...? ' He hesitated.

'Yes?'

'Any time you find me patronising or fussing too much, please tell me at once. Don't bottle it up. Keep the lines of communication open. It's only because I'm concerned about our precious baby.'

She smiled up at him. She had such strong feelings for him now. Stronger than they should be.

The following Wednesday they had a snack on the train so that they could go straight over to see Sebastian. Michel was planning to take her out to dinner somewhere this evening when they got back to St Martin sur Mer. A celebration once they'd seen the scan. Please let it be a celebration, he thought briefly, before banishing the awful thought that it could be otherwise. How on earth did other fathers cope with all the anxiety of pregnancy? As a doctor he should be more laid-back than he was, able to face the outcome of all health situations.

As Sebastian waited for them in his consulting room he couldn't help worrying about his former medical colleague. He'd known Chantal since she'd been a medical student and knew about her trauma last year with Jacques. That fly-by-night doctor who'd spent most of his medical career moving around from hospital to hospital on temporary contracts. The scoundrel had led Chantal to believe all his lies about being single, unattached, in love with her, wanting to marry her.

The entire medical staff who'd worked with Chantal in Paris had been scandalised when the story of Jacques's deception had spread around the grapevine. Everyone had been sympathetic to her but, being the feisty woman she was, sympathy hadn't been what she'd wanted. She'd given in her notice and got herself a position in Emergency at the Hôpital de la Plage, back to her family roots so that she could forget the man who'd betrayed her.

He remembered giving her a glowing reference. The Hôpital de la Plage was a prestigious hospital. There were always many applicants when a post became vacant. He'd had no hesitation in recommending her. The hospital board in Paris hadn't wanted her to leave. They'd hoped she would reconsider her position with them as she had been in line for promotion. But Sebastian had explained the whole sordid story of Jacques's deception.

He'd laid it on thick and had taken great delight in the fact that when Jacques's contract had come up for renewal, his well-timed explanation of the odious man's deception had been one of the reasons the board had refused to renew his contract.

'Your patient is here now,' his receptionist told him over the intercom.

'Make them comfortable in the waiting room. I'll call them in shortly.'

He was still checking the notes in front of him and found himself hoping fervently that Chantal knew what she was doing. He'd had time to make enquiries about her latest boyfriend and had heard nothing but good reports from those in the medical fraternity who'd worked with him. He was a high flyer, excellent at his work, highly intelligent, exceptional at diagnosing difficult cases.

He was a widower who'd been devoted to his wife but unlikely to commit himself to marriage a second time. That worried him a great deal. His wife Susanne, whom he consulted on affairs of the heart, had expressed her concern. She'd advised him to keep an eye on Chantal and make sure she didn't get hurt again.

He went across to open the door, a confident smile in place to reassure Chantal.

'Do come in. How was the journey? You sit here, Chantal, where I can see you. Now, how have you been since I saw you?'

Michel felt very much sidelined. There was an obvious bond of friendship between Chantal and Sebastian. That was good from the point of view that he would take special care of her. He himself had to realise that he'd done very little towards creating this pregnancy and what he'd achieved had been from a purely natural and immensely wonderful experience. So, for once in his life he had to learn to take a back seat.

There was some discussion about blood tests and haemoglobin levels. Sebastian was pleased with her general good health. He touched briefly on Chantal's miscarriage, which had happened the previous September.

Yes, his records showed that she'd had a spontaneous miscarriage thought to have been triggered by the stress of the situation she'd found herself in. Subsequently she'd had a D and C to make sure that the inside of the uterus was healthy again and would be viable for any future pregnancy.

Chantal listened impassively to Sebastian recapping her medical history. She wanted to forget the past and move on to this pregnancy. So precious because she'd never expected it would happen to her again.

Michel was relieved to hear that she'd been well cared for after the miscarriage but he was also anxious to see the scan of their baby.

A nurse came in from the treatment room to say she was ready to do the scan whenever required.

Michel placed his hand on Chantal's waist as they walked into the treatment room together. She found the touch of his hand reassuring. They were in this together. He was being protective towards her. If anything showed up on the ultrasound that was a problem, she could take it if Michel was with her.

He was helping her up onto the couch now. She gave him a grateful smile for his help and also for being there with her because she suddenly felt scared. She'd had to assume there would be no problems with this pregnancy. But until now there'd been nothing to reassure her.

The nurse was rubbing the gel on her abdomen. At three months pregnant Chantal hadn't detected any roundness or swelling.

She looked up at the screen above the treatment couch. Sebastian was giving a running commentary as they started the scan. Everything was in its rightful place, no abnormalities.

'And here it is, the tiny foetus.'

Sebastian couldn't contain his excitement. He'd never been able to do the first viewing of an unborn baby without feeling it.

Chantal grabbed Michel's hand. 'Look, Michel, our baby. Oh, will somebody take a picture, please?'

'That's all under control,' Sebastian told her. 'We'll give you a picture to take home when— Hang on a minute…'

'What's the matter?' Michel said, anxiously. 'Oh, I see! There's a second foetus, isn't there?'

'Yes, there are two of them,' Sebastian announced solemnly. 'Congratulations, both of you! You're expecting twins.'

Chantal stared at the two shapes that were barely discernible on the screen but they were her twin babies, their twin babies. She gripped Michel's hand more tightly as she turned to look at him. She saw the tears in his eyes beginning to roll down his cheeks as their eyes met. She would never forget this precious moment. For the rest of her life she would remember the moment she'd known for certain that she was going to be a mother.

Michel turned his eyes back to the screen. He needed a private moment to share with those two unborn babies. His love for them was almost too much to bear. And he could feel his admiration and affection for the mother of his children strengthening. As he watched these living babies that they'd made together he felt a strong bond growing between them. A powerful emotion was challenging all his previous ideas.

CHAPTER TEN

HE REACHED FOR her hand across the table. She smiled as his fingers curled around hers. Watching the scan of their babies that afternoon had been a truly moving experience for her and she knew Michel had felt exactly the same. Probably more so, from his emotional reaction. He was a real softie at heart, an absolute pussy cat. She couldn't have believed when she'd first met him in February that he could change so much when she got to know him.

She realised she'd also changed during the last few months. It was pure determination that made her hold out for her independence. Her feelings for Michel were too deep and complicated to analyse. She didn't want to give in to the emotional changes that were taking place in her mind. If she'd wanted a more desirable father for her baby it wouldn't have been possible to find one.

She could hear the little voice that spoke to her constantly in her head as she tried so hard to ignore her strong emotional feelings for Michel. Why was she still so afraid of losing her independence? Michel wasn't like Jacques. Every instinct she had was telling her that he was totally honest. She could depend on him one hundred per cent in any situation. But Michel's whole concern was to become a father. No one could replace Maxine.

He was holding her hand now out of gratitude that she'd made fatherhood possible for him.

As Michel continued to hold Chantal's hand he was also thinking about the scan of their babies that afternoon. The strong emotions that had moved him as he'd seen them on screen. He could feel the pain of losing Maxine fading in the face of new life and found that he was becoming more and more caught up in his feelings for Chantal.

'Are you OK, Michel?'

He smiled at her. 'I'm fine. Never better. I think I'm overwhelmed by the scan of our babies this afternoon. I can't stop thinking about it.'

He stopped himself from becoming too effusive. He mustn't get carried away while his emotions were so difficult to understand.

He signalled for the bill. 'We shouldn't stay out too late. It's been a long day for you.'

'And you,' she said, with a wry smile.

'Yes, but I'm not…sorry. Am I being too concerned about you?'

'I'm getting used to it and finding it very charming. Outside of working hours, that is.'

'I think you should take the morning off tomorrow. No, hear me out.' He avoided telling her it was an order, aware that she disliked the word. 'In fact, I'm going to insist and authorise the whole day off for you.'

As they walked outside to the car she didn't demur. She *was* feeling tired. and Michel was quite right. She should take care of herself.

He didn't start the car immediately but simply leaned across and put his arm on the back of her seat. 'I hope you approved of my choice of restaurant tonight?'

'Very smart. Expensive, I should imagine.'

'Nothing too good for the mother of my children.'

'And easier to get to than the beach café.'

He smiled down into her eyes. 'You might be too heavy for me to carry over the sand! Joking aside, you don't look any different. Hard to believe there are two babies in there.'

'It was like a miracle.'

As they sat very still, both engrossed in their own thoughts, Michel could feel the emotional rapport growing between them.

'I've got a proposition to put to you,' he said gently. 'I'd like you to come back home with me tonight so that I can show you the changes I've made since I knew I was going to be a father. I've prepared a bedroom that will be yours to use whenever you want to use it. There's another room beside it that we can use as a nursery. Obviously we'll need to employ a trained nurse to take care of our babies if you choose to go back to work.'

'Michel, I really haven't thought so far ahead.' She paused as she saw the disappointed expression on his face. 'Let's discuss that another time, shall we? But I'd love to go back to your house to see the changes you've made,' she added hastily, so as not to hurt his feelings.

Suddenly she felt that events were going too quickly for her. It had only been a few weeks ago that she'd agreed to have a baby with Michel, even though she'd only known him for a short time and that had been as colleagues.

Now she had two babies on the way, which was wonderful, but the trappings that inevitably went with parenthood had all got to be finalised in the next few months. She would try to take it one step at a time. Michel's endless enthusiasm was great to witness but exhausting when he tried to rush her along with him.

She made allowances for the fact that as the director of Emergency he had to think on his feet, make split-second life-and-death decisions. He was perfect in his professional work.

But domestic life wasn't like that. At least, not in her experience. Were they really going to be compatible during the long years of parenthood ahead of them?

As he started the engine he knew he'd only told her half of what was in his mind. 'Of course, if you prefer to go back to your poky little room in the medics' quarters, spend your off duty confined within those four small walls…'

She gave him a deliberately whimsical smile 'OK, I've got the message. I must say it's very tempting.'

Michel smiled happily. So far so good. As he changed gear to go up the hill he was already planning ahead what he should say. If she approved of the room he'd prepared, would she give him an answer to the question that was uppermost in his mind? He didn't want her to feel she was losing her independence so he must reassure her he would give her space in their new situation together.

'It's a lovely room, Michel.'

'I'm glad you like it.'

He walked across and pushed open a door that led through to a smaller room, which was completely devoid of furniture.

'I had all the furniture taken out because I thought this could be the nursery. And now we know we're going to have twins you can choose their cots and the furniture you would like to go in here. There's a baby furniture shop in St Martin but maybe you'd prefer to go up to Paris to select what's needed? If I'm honest…'

He took a deep breath. 'It would be a great relief if you'd move in here. I would know you and the babies were being well cared for. You'd get away from hospital and have more space and comfort. We could make plans for the future. And when the babies were born you would be used to the house. What do you say?'

Her mind was spinning with the enormity of this new situation. Michel was being very generous and considerate but his main concern was the welfare of his babies. As she'd passed the photos in the hall on her way up here she'd known she mustn't commit herself to any situation that could result in losing her independence to a man who was in love with someone else. She hadn't known that Jacques had a wife. This time she knew where Michel's heart lay and she couldn't compete with a ghost.

'To be honest, Michel, I'm too tired to think about anything except sleep tonight. So if you don't mind…'

His brow furrowed. 'Of course you must rest now. I had the bed made up in your room because I knew you'd be tired. I'll be right next door if you need anything.'

On impulse she turned to hold out her arms towards him. He'd gone to so much trouble. He was prepared to pander to her every whim.

'Thank you, Michel,' she whispered, her voice barely discernible as she clung to him, unable to cope with the conflicting emotions that were running through her.

He could feel her body quivering as they stood together. It was all he could do not to scoop her up into his arms and carry her to his bed, to make love to her all night as he'd done the night their precious babies were conceived. But wonderful as that would be, it wouldn't solve the problem of their future together.

She pulled herself away from his warm embrace, not allowing herself to respond to the feelings she'd had as he'd held her close.

'Goodnight, Michel.'

He bent his head and gave her a brief kiss before turning away and leaving the room.

It was ages before he could sleep. He put on his bedside light and plumped up his pillows so he could lie back and read if he couldn't sleep. He could check on the report he was writing for tomorrow's board meeting.

He tried to concentrate but he couldn't as his thoughts turned inevitably back to Chantal.

He got out of bed and padded barefoot over to the window that led to the balcony. He pulled his robe around him. It felt decidedly chilly out there in the early hours of the morning. Everything was supposed to seem more difficult before the dawn. That was certainly true of his thoughts about their complicated relationship. He should be the happiest man alive knowing that he was soon to be father of twins. And yet he couldn't help wanting to have Chantal close by him. He enjoyed being with her.

He hoped she was warm enough in the room next door. Of course she was! She would be fast asleep, tucked up in the new bed.

Was he moving things along too fast? Was that why she seemed so far away from him at times, wrapped up in her own thoughts? Should he have consulted her first before building the little nest for their babies?

Chantal had lain awake after Michel had left her. The idea of having her own room in his house, complete with nursery for their babies, was very tempting. It was what Michel wanted. She thought of the plans they'd drawn up at the beginning of their unconventional scheme. Parenthood had just been a word then. Now it was a reality. It was a lifelong commitment. She'd known that from the beginning but she hadn't thought it through.

She had to admit that if she wanted a lifelong commitment then Michel was the man she would choose. It was the institution of being tied to another person that scared her. But she already had his babies inside her. That was binding enough, wasn't it? Why fight against the warm feelings she had towards the father of her babies? She couldn't ignore these disturbingly strong emotional feelings towards him. If she was honest with herself she would say she was in danger of falling in love with him. Maybe she already had but wouldn't admit it.

She sat up and switched on the light, looking around the room, this beautifully appointed room that Michel had prepared for her. She could be happy here. She could go one further and admit that she would be even happier to be in Michel's bed at this moment. She felt so safe when she was with him. So sure that the physical desires she felt for him were what she wanted.

But Michel was still in love with Maxine and in any case he'd said he would never commit to a loving relationship that might end prematurely and leave him utterly bereft. She must stop fantasising and consider the facts. She should keep her independence. Stick to the original plan and stop becoming carried away with romantic ideas that weren't viable. She was going to be a mother to two babies. That was all she wanted.

She was awakened by the sound of knocking on her door. Michel was carrying a tray. He put it down on the bedside table.

'I've got to leave soon.'

He was being deliberately brusque to counteract his real feelings at the sight of her beautiful long dark hair spread out across the pillow. What he really wanted was for her to hold out her arms and invite him into her bed. Perhaps if he appeared unavailable it would make her want him.

He hovered by the bedside for a few moments until he admitted his reverse psychology wasn't working on her.

He cleared his throat. 'Make sure you rest today, Chantal. Call me if there's something you need, won't you?'

'Of course.' She smiled up at him. 'Thank you for the coffee and the croissant.'

'Straight out of the freezer into the high-speed oven. Hope it's thawed out enough. See you tonight.'

He made a quick exit in case he changed his mind and made suggestions that he might regret.

She reached for her coffee, wondering why he was in such a rush. She'd barely woken up. She'd hoped he might join her for breakfast at least. Looking across at the window, the silky curtains held back at the sides by golden tassels, she remembered that she had a whole day to pamper herself.

First she took a long bath, sprinkling some of the contents of the bottle of scented bath foam liberally into the water. When she finally decided that she should make a move she reached for one of the large fluffy towels.

As she wrapped it round her she had the disturbing feeling that she was in a luxury hotel. All well and good for a visit but could she ever call it home? Was this what she wanted for her babies?

A couple of weeks passed during which time the crucial question of where she should live when the babies were born was never too far from her mind. She found herself working hard, trying to blot out the doubts that taunted her when she had time to think.

Michel was as attentive as usual towards her when they were working together but in a more professional way. He'd taken the hint that she didn't want his attentions to overwhelm her. He reined in his anxious feelings that she was working too hard. As he noticed her coming out of a cubicle, having dealt with a patient and now prepared to take on another, he couldn't help himself from intervening. Swiftly he strode across the floor.

'Chantal, may I have a word?'

He spoke briefly first to the nurse who was trying to summon Chantal over to her cubicle, telling her he would deal with the problem himself.

'It's lunchtime, Chantal,' he said, quietly.

'I'm not hungry. I'll take a break shortly.'

'You may not be hungry but our babies need you to have regular feeds, don't they?'

He whispered this, knowing it wouldn't be well received.

'And you're looking particularly tired this morning. Try and have some rest when you've had lunch. I'll cover for you if you're late back. I've been thinking it might be a good idea for you to work part time soon. What do you think?'

She drew in her breath. She didn't dare to tell him what she thought at this moment. It wouldn't be good for their precious babies if she allowed herself to let fling the expletives that came to mind.

As she turned and headed for the medics' dining room she suddenly realised that Michel had been quite right. She had been feeling particularly tired this morning and there was a dragging feeling in the lower regions of her abdomen. She made a detour to the women's toilets.

Reaching for the push button to flush the loo, she looked in horror at the tell-tale signs of blood in the lavatory bowl. She put her hand to her mouth to stifle the cry that rose in her throat as she felt blood trickling down between her legs.

'No, no! Not again!'

CHAPTER ELEVEN

SHE LAY VERY still in the small room off the obstetrics prenatal ward. Everything had happened so quickly. One minute she'd felt reasonably OK and the next she'd found she was being loaded onto a trolley and brought up here to Obstetrics.

Michel was sitting beside her, anxious for the obstetrics consultant to arrive.

'Pierre's still in Theatre,' he told her, relaying the message he'd just received.

Genevieve came to ask how she was feeling now that she'd been settled in a bed. She came over and checked the large pad between Chantal's legs.

'Mmm,' was all she said as she changed it.

Michel had left the room to give them some privacy.

'Do you think the bleeding is slowing down, Genevieve?'

'It will take a while before we can assess what's happening, Chantal. Don't get out of bed. Lie as still as you can. Pierre Marchand will be here as soon as he can get away from Theatre.'

Minutes later he arrived, still in his theatre greens.

Chantal stared up at him, anxious to hear his assessment of her condition. Her heart was beating more rapidly than it should as she remained convinced it was happening to her again. This was exactly like the last time, except she'd been totally alone when she'd miscarried last September. This time she had her baby's father anxiously hovering at the back of the room.

She glanced across and gave him a smile of reassurance, even though she didn't feel there was much hope. In the half-hour since the nurse in the ladies room who'd heard her scream had alerted Michel it had become obvious that nobody on the medical staff had been unaware of their unconventional relationship. But the fact that she was pregnant, or possibly that she had been pregnant, added another dimension to their supposedly secret liaison.

She tried to relax as Pierre examined her. He straightened up, his expression   enigmatic.

'We'll need a scan, Sister.' He looked down at Chantal. 'I'll have you taken down to the treatment room as soon as possible, Chantal. If things look OK, we'll treat you here with complete bed rest for a few days until things settle down again. If the pregnancy isn't viable...'

Pierre paused, not wanting to upset her any more than she appeared to be. He'd been briefed that his patient had miscarried with her first pregnancy last September.

'It's OK, Pierre,' Chantal said quietly. 'I'm prepared for the worst-case scenario. If the pregnancy isn't viable you would perform a D and C, I presume?'

The obstetrician nodded. 'Yes, but let's stay positive until we find out what's happening, Chantal.'

Michel moved forward and took hold of Chantal's hand. He may be the father of these babies but he felt as if he was getting in the way of the expert Obstetrics team.

She clung to Michel's hand.

'I'm so glad you're here,' she whispered.

He found his spirits lifting. She wanted him; she needed him. He was already thinking of the worst-case scenario. If that happened, would she stay with him so they could try again? His affection for her was growing stronger every day. In fact, he couldn't imagine life without her now.

Michel had a quick word with Pierre before leaving the room. Out in the corridor he switched on his mobile and punched in Sebastian's private number at the Paris clinic.

'I'll come over,' Sebastian said tersely as soon as Michel had given him the stark facts.

Michel tried to convince him that Chantal was in good hands. Pierre Marchand was an excellent obstetrician, but Sebastian insisted that Chantal was his patient and had also been a personal friend of his family for many years. He would be with them towards the end of the afternoon so that he could liaise with Pierre, their Obstetrician. It was important that if Chantal was having a miscarriage she have expert attention to determine the cause of two miscarriages. This would ensure that her next pregnancy had more of a chance of being successful.

'One baby here,' Pierre pointed out as Chantal and Michel gazed at the screen.

'Another one hiding behind it, here,' Michel said, his voice choking with emotion and relief. His babies were still alive, but would they stay so till full term? What was the significance of this bleeding?

'Complete rest is needed, Chantal.'

Pierre spoke with the authority of a consultant who'd had to stress this to patients before. He turned to look at

Michel. 'We must ensure that Chantal rests completely. The next few days are crucial. She mustn't get out of bed. All we can do is wait to see if the bleeding stops. Continue with the glucose saline infusion until the condition stabilises. Keep me informed please.'

Michel explained that Chantal's obstetrician was coming over from Paris to liaise with him. Pierre had no quarrel with that.

'Two heads are better than one. Only the best for our important patient.'

Chantal was delighted when Sebastian walked into her room. She was even more pleased to see that he was accompanied by Susanne. They had all been friends for many years.

Sebastian asked if he could see their obstetrician for a full report as soon as possible.

Michel, who'd been with Chantal all afternoon, put a call through to Pierre, who arrived shortly afterwards. The two obstetricians agreed that complete rest was necessary until Chantal was out of danger. The cause of the loss of blood hadn't been ascertained yet.

'Were you worrying about something, Chantal?' Sebastian asked, gently.

He glanced across at his wife as he waited for his patient's reply. They had their own theory about this unconventional relationship that Chantal was involved in. They'd discussed it at length on the way over from Paris.

Chantal hesitated. 'Nothing in particular,' she said carefully, aware that now she was even more the centre of attention in this small, crowded room. Instinctively she knew what Sebastian and Susanne were thinking. They'd brought up four children in a conventional, loving marriage. She'd known at her first professional appointment in Paris that Sebastian would be concerned about the unconventional situation between Michel and herself.

'Nothing at all?' Sebastian prompted gently.

She steeled herself and wouldn't be drawn as she told herself this relationship would work. They would make it work.

She shook her head. 'Michel and I have got everything in place ready for our twins. There's even a well-equipped nursery in Michel's house. When I go back to work after out babies are born we're going to employ a trained nurse to take care of them when we're both on duty at the same time.'

Susanne moved forward from the back of the room where she'd been watching quietly.

'Don't go back to work too early, my dear. I spent time at home after the birth of all four of our babies. It's a precious time to bond with them.'

Pierre seemed impatient now. 'With respect, *Madame*, childcare isn't under discussion now. Especially when we cannot be sure that these babies will go to full term. We have to be realistic. Chantal has assured us she's not having to worry about anything. Michel will be a devoted father. Sebastian and I both agree that at the moment we have to ensure complete rest for our patient.'

Susanne cleared her throat. 'Have you contacted your mother, Chantal?'

'She's still on holiday on the coast near Bordeaux. I didn't want to worry her.'

'How about your cousin who lives inland from here?'

'I was planning to contact Julia when we knew for certain whether the pregnancy is still viable.'

'The pregnancy will have more of a chance of being

viable if we allow our patient to rest now,' Pierre suggested dryly. 'Let's keep in touch, Sebastian, but for the moment I think we should give Chantal the chance to rest.'

In the middle of the night Chantal woke up, initially confused about where she was. She felt somehow different. There was a small light in the corner of the room and a nurse was sitting in an armchair, reading. She stood up and came across the room.

'How are you feeling, Chantal?'

'I think I'm OK.'

'I'll check your pad while you're awake. I last checked two hours ago.' The nurse smiled. 'It's dry, not a sign of blood. Excellent!'

Chantal felt a huge sense of relief. 'I'd love to think my babies are safe now but I know it's early days.'

The nurse nodded. 'Dr Marchand usually puts his patients on at least two weeks complete rest when they've got a threatened miscarriage, especially when they've already suffered one before.'

'Yes, but during my last miscarriage I was in a completely different situation,' she said quietly, almost to herself. 'My obstetrician last September told me that the unpleasant experience I'd been through had triggered my miscarriage.

The nurse was adjusting the speed of the glucose saline infusion 'That does happen,' she agreed quietly. 'Now, please try not to think about it. Try to sleep again. Does my light disturb you?'

'No. It's comforting to know I'm not alone. Last time I was.'

She wouldn't think about the past. Only positive

thoughts from now on. She was going to be fine. Her babies would survive.

She closed her eyes, pretending to be asleep so she didn't have to talk any more. It would soon be morning. She'd ring Julia, check on how her cousin's pregnancy was going along. She hadn't seen her for a few weeks.

She found herself wondering how Michel was. She'd had to persuade him that it wasn't necessary for him to miss his sleep. He'd agreed to leave her only when he'd made her promise to contact him if there was any change. He wasn't going home, though. He would be in his usual room in the medics quarters, close at hand if she needed him.

The sun was stealing over the windowsill when she next woke up. She'd made it through the night. The nurse checked her pad for signs of blood. Still dry but she must remain in bed.

It was mid-morning before she rang Julia. Michel had been in to see her and had gone away to organise the staff in the emergency department. He would be back shortly when he was satisfied they could manage without him.

Pierre had been in to see her and had been pleased with the news that the bleeding had stopped. He was going to liaise with Sebastian over the phone and keep him in the picture.

Julia's line was busy. She left a message. Minutes later her cousin rang back and they chatted happily. Chantal relaxed against her pillows. It was always good to talk to her cousin. They immediately struck up the familiar rapport that existed between them and became the two excitable young girls they'd been in the past.

'How are you, Julia? I Haven't seen you for weeks.'

'I'm as big as a house! I'm due at the end of the month.

Can't wait to be delivered. Bernard and I don't get out much when he's not lecturing his students or supervising their efforts in the operating theatre. And he's still got patients to see when he's not teaching.

'He's so nervous about me being pregnant. Honestly, you wouldn't think he was a doctor. If this was how he treated his patients they'd all complain. Talk about wrapping me in cotton wool!'

Chantal was giggling already at her cousin's description of Bernard as an anxious father. He always seemed such a confident man when she saw him in hospital but, then, so did Michel.

'Julia, I know exactly what you mean.'

'Oh, you've no idea what I'm talking about, Chantal. You've absolutely no idea…or have you?'

Julia stopped in mid-flow. 'Chantal, is there something you haven't told me? What did you mean just now?'

'I was going to tell you the next time we met up but I've been so busy and…'

'You're not…you're not…?'

'I am! Yes, I'm pregnant.'

There was a whoop of excitement at the other end. Chantal held her mobile at arm's length till the deafening cries died down.

'I'm glad you're pleased, Julia.'

'Pleased? I've over the moon for you. I assume it's Michel's.'

'How did you guess?'

'Oh, come on, it's obvious. You two were made for each other!'

'Well, it's not quite like that. It's a bit unconventional,' she said cautiously. 'You see, we only got together because we both wanted a baby and even then… Oh , I'll explain what happened and what was meant to happen when I see you. Too complicated to tell you over the phone so don't ask. Actually, it's twins.'

'Wonderful, even better! Can't wait to hear the details when we get together. Our twin mothers will be pleased you're keeping up the family tradition. Have you told your mother yet?'

'Hold on a minute, Julia. I haven't dared to tell her. I'm actually in the obstetrics ward under the care of Pierre Marchand. I had some bleeding so I'm confined to bed rest. I've had a scan and the babies are fine but we're not out of the woods yet.'

'Oh, I'm so sorry. You poor thing, cooped up in hospital. Tell you what, why don't I get Bernard to come down and talk to Pierre? They're good friends and Bernard will persuade him you need to be pampered among your own family. You should be up here at the farm with us. How far gone are you?'

'About three and a half months.'

'My, my, you kept that quiet, didn't you? We definitely need to catch up on this complicated and top secret pregnancy, don't we?'

'Julia, are you sure you want me to impose myself on you at this late stage in your pregnancy? You've got enough on your plate with taking care of Philippe and everything else you have to do up at the farm.'

'Chantal, I'm bored out of my tiny mind. Marianne does everything for Philippe, Bernard and, of course, me. She practically spoon-feeds me at mealtimes, standing over me to check I'm eating my greens. "Good for the baby!" That's all I hear.

'She'll be delighted to have a real patient to fuss over. We've got everything up here in the farmhouse, ancient bedpans, voluminous nightdresses for pregnant ladies,

nutritious food from the farm, expert doctors on hand to
check anything you'd like checked.'

Julia broke off for a moment to speak to Bernard, who
was just arriving in the room.

'Come here a moment, it's Chantal. When you get
yourself into hospital this morning we'd like you to speak
to Pierre Marchand. Chantal, I'll call you back when I've
explained the situation to Bernard. Take care of yourself.
See you soon!'

CHAPTER TWELVE

'MICHEL, YOU'VE GOT to believe that Chantal will get the best attention up here at the farm with Julia and me.'

Bernard was doing his best to convince Michel, his colleague and friend at the hospital, that they only had Chantal's best interests at heart.

Chantal lay back against her pillows, trying to stay calm. She was merely the patient and had no say in her treatment apparently. The argument was purely academic now anyway. Bernard had brought her up to the farm to be with Julia. As far as Chantal was concerned, she was here now and here she was going to stay.

She'd assumed that Pierre would have informed Michel but apparently he'd been in Theatre and the message hadn't got through to him. As soon as he'd got Pierre's message Michel had come racing up to the farm to enquire what was going on.

She remembered that when she had been in the obstetrics side ward Michel had suggested it would be safer for her to move in with him. She knew he was naturally feeling protective of her, but was that enough for her to give up her independence? His main concern was obviously for the welfare of his babies. She was merely the vessel that was carrying them.

A couple of hours ago she'd listened to Bernard convincing Pierre that being with Julia and himself at the farm would be the best scenario for their patient. They were all doctors so there would be no shortage of medical attention if Chantal started to bleed again. It would also help her to be with her cousin, away from hospital in the healthy surroundings of the farm amongst the hills.

Julia decided it was her turn to up speak up. 'I entirely agree that it's better Chantal is here with family, rather than spending her time resting—or rather, trying to rest—in the hospital. Michel, you're welcome to come and stay here any time you like. Consider yourself part of the family now that you and Chantal are expecting twins together. And if I'm totally honest, as I'm now nearing the conclusion of my pregnancy I would really like my cousin to be here with me.'

Michel reached for Chantal's hand. 'What do you want, Chantal?'

At last they were all going to listen to her opinion. 'I'm grateful to Bernard that he persuaded Pierre to let me out of hospital to be here with Julia. That's exactly what I want.'

Michel leaned forward and drew her into his arms as Bernard and Julia left them to be alone together.

'So long as this is best for the babies and you, I'm happy,' he said gently.

She found the feeling of his arms holding her was very comforting. It was also stirring up memories of that night when they'd made the babies together.

He looked into her eyes. She loved the sincere expression in his. He was a good man, a sexy, alluring man. She was lucky to be in a partnership with him, even if he was there only because of the babies. Right now she could imagine it was for real but she had to face the facts of their unorthodox liaison. She listened to his deeply caring voice as he tried to reassure her that all would be well.

Michel drew her closer in his arms. 'I'll come to see you every day. Pierre thinks you'll be fine if you have complete rest for a couple of weeks. If you'd taken up my suggestion to move into my house I could have arranged for you to be nursed at home in your own room. I could have employed a trained nurse and also taken some time off to take care of you. I've already made enquiries at a reputable agency about employing a trained nurse to help you at home in the prenatal and postnatal stages.'

'You're very kind, Michel, but I like being with family here. It's more relaxing for me, more homely. Julia and I grew up together like sisters.'

Whenever Michel spoke about his home, that magnificent house overlooking the bay of St Martin, she felt worried. Events were moving too fast for her. She was being carried along on a tidal wave with little control over events. She was still overjoyed at the thought that she was carrying twins but apprehensive about all the trappings of the unusual parenthood that went with it.

'If you're happy to be here at the farm with Bernard and Julia then I'll stop worrying about you.'

She moved in his arms. His lips brushed hers tentatively as if he wasn't sure she would welcome him. She felt a rush of sensual excitement at the touch of his lips but he was already pulling away before she could respond.

She remained still in his arms, moved by the expression of affection on his handsome face. She told herself he loved the babies, not her. The love of his life would always be Maxine.

'Chantal, I've been so worried about you and the babies,' he said huskily.

She remained silent as she tried to make sense of her confused thoughts. 'Michel, it's been traumatic for both of us, believing that we might lose our babies.'

'And I was terrified I might lose you when you first started to bleed. Until the bleeding stopped I couldn't bear to be away from you.'

He broke off, not wanting to upset Chantal with the thoughts that had plagued him. He'd reviewed all the rare cases he'd witnessed during his career. To lose someone you really cared about was the worst thing that could happen to anyone.

'Michel, we're both in a highly emotional state at the moment. Once I'm fit again we'll review our future plans for the babies, get ourselves back on course with our original plan. Make it work.'

He stood up. 'Of course the plan will work.' He spoke decisively but he realised that his emotions were changing all the time. The babies were at the forefront of his mind but so was their mother, this wonderful woman for whom he felt such strong affection. But he knew he mustn't question their original plan for non-commitment to each other. Chantal valued her independence above everything else.

Chantal also was feeling confused at the strengthening attraction she felt towards him. But these strong feelings she felt for him now would disappear when life became normal again. She was simply feeling fragile and clingy after her threatened miscarriage.

'You must rest now,' he said, in a calm, controlled, almost professional way, the doctor in him regarding what the patient needed most. 'I've got to go back to hospital to see the patient I was operating on when Pierre allowed you to come up here. I'll come and see you tomorrow, if you'd like me to?'

'Of course I want you to come and see me!' She put out her arms as he leaned down towards her. She found herself clinging to him, wishing he would stay, but he was already pulling away, intent on getting back to the hospital where he understood exactly what was going on. Being in this intense, emotional atmosphere was confusing. Would he ever understand what went on inside Chantal's mind?

Would she be with him long enough for him to find out? She was so beautiful, so very attractive. He'd seen the admiring glances that other men gave when they looked at her. There was nothing to stop her having a relationship with another man in the future. He couldn't bear that to happen!

Chantal closed her eyes after he'd gone. She heard his footsteps receding on the stairs then the sound of his car engine starting up. What was this yearning to be close to Michel but then finding it impossible to commit herself to him for ever? For ever was a long time and people changed over the years.

She took deep breaths to calm herself. Yes, she should rest for the sake of their babies. She had to stop worrying about the future.

Michel realised he was driving too fast when he had to brake hard at the hairpin bend halfway down the hill. The lorry coming slowly up the hill veered out of the way at the same time as he did.

He breathed a sigh of relief as he let in the clutch and moved on again, this time more slowly. He hadn't expected that huge lorry to be taking up more than half the road. But that was no excuse for him being totally wrapped up in his own thoughts.

He reached the bottom of the hill and was still plagued by his dilemma in spite of trying desperately to concentrate on his driving. He was on the straight section of road now that led to the hospital. As he relaxed he couldn't help his thoughts turning to Chantal again.

He'd never thought he could love another woman after Maxine had died but his feelings for Chantal were now becoming very strong. He hesitated to call it love, still feeling he was being untrue to Maxine's memory. But was it possible to love two women, one who was here and one who was now a much-loved memory?

He turned into the hospital gates. He must concentrate on work now. Chantal was staying for two weeks with Julia and Bernard and would be well cared for. He must remain as unemotional as he could so that her convalescence would be successful.

Julia came into her room next morning soon after Chantal had woken up. Waiting outside the half-open door, she could see Bernard and Philippe.

'I know it's early for visitors but Philippe so wanted to see you before he went to school and Bernard is waiting to drive him there.'

'Philippe!'

Chantal was very fond of her step-nephew, who came across to give his favourite aunt a kiss.

She remarked on how tall he was now.

'I'm seven,' he told her proudly. 'And I'm going on an expedition today with my class. It's still summer holidays but our class are old enough to go on a geography field trip.'

He chatted on excitedly about the day ahead.

Marianne arrived, carrying a breakfast tray.

'We'll have to go now, Philippe,' Bernard told his son. 'Mustn't miss the coach.'

'I'm afraid it's decaf coffee,' Julia told her cousin as she lowered herself into a large armchair. 'Bernard doesn't approve of real coffee during pregnancy. Once I've delivered this precious baby and breastfed him for a few months I can please myself again.'

'So it's a boy?'

'Yes, I'm carrying a boy. But don't tell Philippe because he'll expect to be able to play with him from day one. I'm leaving the good news as a surprise.'

'They're bossy, aren't they?' Chantal remarked as she took a sip of the decaf coffee, which was generously laced with hot milk.

Julia shifted herself in the armchair as she tried to get comfortable.

'Do you mean expectant fathers in general or just ours?'

Chantal smiled. 'Probably just ours. I think it's because they're both doctors and know all about what's best for the patient.'

'Or *think* they do,' her cousin put in dryly, handing Julia a warm croissant on a plate. 'Here you go. Try not to make as many crumbs in the bed as you usually do.'

They were both giggling now, as they'd done so many times when they'd been small.

'Chantal, I used to think you deliberately made a mess of your breakfast so that you could get some attention from whichever mother was in charge at the time.'

'You're probably right. When both mothers were chatting the whole time I had to do something to be noticed.'

Julia finished her croissant first and reached for another one. 'I'm glad you've found a good man this time, after what you went through last time. I think you and Michel make an ideal couple.'

Chantal put the remains of her croissant on the plate. 'We're not really a couple, you know, not in the conventional sense.'

'Well, you could have fooled me! So how did you get pregnant, by mail order?'

'Mmm, we had a night of wild passionate love.' Chantal lay back against the pillows as the wonderful memories of that night came flooding back to her. 'It was the most wonderful experience I've ever lived through.'

Julia remained silent for a few moments. 'So, you're in love, aren't you?'

'Julia, I honestly don't know. I was so traumatised after Jacques deceived me I promised myself I would never give myself to another man as long as I lived. Once you commit to someone you open yourself up to being vulnerable and I don't want that.'

'But Michel isn't like Jacques, Chantal. He's a good man, honest, caring and very sexy, impossibly handsome! You couldn't have anyone better in your life. And what's most important, I can tell he adores you.'

'But how do I know that's not simply because I'm carrying his babies? Love, adoration, call it what you like, is an impossible emotion to understand. How do I know that because he's affectionate towards me that it's true love? And even if it is love, how do I know his love will stand the test of time?'

Julia put down her coffee cup and became deadly serious. 'You don't know. Chantal; you've got to trust your instincts and go with the flow. Life changes all the time.

'Last September you set yourself cast-iron rules that would stop you being hurt in the future. But you hadn't met Michel then. You've got to be more flexible. Take life as it comes. Adapt yourself to this new situation you're in. I had to make new decisions about life when Bernard and I were sorting out our differences and I've never been happier.'

Chantal swallowed hard. 'But I'm so confused.'

'So was I, but you've got to make a decision about your relationship soon. If Michel doesn't know how you feel about him he may stick to the idea of a partnership for the sake of the babies. Don't let that happen! Once you totally commit yourself you'll know that was the right course of action. You'll find a way to make it work. Believe me, Chantal, you will.'

The next few days were passing very quickly and Chantal could feel herself getting stronger. Pierre came out to see her a couple of times and phoned every day to check on how she was. As she'd had no further bleeding during the second week, she was allowed out of bed.

Michel came to see her at some point every day, staying for a couple of hours or longer if he had the time. Chantal found herself looking forward to seeing him. She could feel her heart pounding as he bounded up the stairs, moving swiftly across the room to kiss her. But she sensed he was holding something back as they sat side by side in armchairs by the window.

Julia always came in at some point, knocking on the door before she came in. She didn't ask questions after Michel had gone. But Chantal had confided in her that she was glad she had time to herself to think about the future between Michel's visits.

'So, have you had any profound thoughts about your future, Chantal?' Julia asked as they sat together by the window on the day before she was due to leave the farm.

Chantal could feel the warm afternoon sun shining through the wide open French window. She'd been dreading telling her cousin what she'd decided but the decision she'd made after much deliberation seemed the most rational.

'Yes, I've made my decision.' She hesitated. 'I've seen a distinct change in Michel's attitude towards me ever since he saw the scan of the babies. I can't rule out the idea that he's fallen in love with the concept of being a father.'

'Well, of course he has. That's normal. But he also loves you. That's obvious.'

'I'm still very sceptical.' She took a deep breath. 'So I'm not going to renew my contract, which comes up for discussion next week.'

Julia sat still, silently fuming. She knew her cousin better than anyone. She could be so stubborn when she was convinced she was right. This time she was definitely wrong but how could she persuade her otherwise when she could see her mind was made up?

'I'm going to go back to my apartment in Paris and make preparations for the birth of my babies. Maybe I'll arrange to go back to work part time in my old job at the hospital until the babies are born.'

'Chantal, you may change your mind about being on your own.'

'Mum will be next door and…please, Julia, I'm trying to be rational, not emotional, in not committing my fate to someone else.'

'I don't want to upset you, Chantal,' Julia said in a quiet, resigned tone. 'If that's your decision I'll help you all I can.' She hesitated. 'Did you tell Michel your plans when he was here this morning?'

'No, I thought I would tell him tomorrow. He's planning to collect me in the afternoon and take me up to his house. I thought it would be better if we were by ourselves when I tell him.'

'Oh, it's a good idea that you should be alone when you drop your bombshell.'

'Julia, I'm having his babies. That's what we agreed on at the beginning, nothing more, nothing less. We'll draw up a legal contract together and I'll keep to it.'

Julia didn't trust herself to speak. She eased herself out of the chair and walked back to her room. Her cousin could be so difficult when she wanted to be. She had always been stubborn but never as bad as this before that dreadful Jacques had caused her so much pain. He had a lot to answer for.

CHAPTER THIRTEEN

JULIA HAD LAIN awake for a long time during the night, worrying about what Chantal had told her. She'd known exactly what the poor girl was going through in her confusing dilemma to sort out her emotional feelings for Michel. She'd been in the same situation before she'd married Bernard. She should have given her cousin some sound advice from her own experience, not just walked away, leaving her to struggle by herself.

But Chantal wasn't listening to any of her advice now so her words of advice would have fallen on deaf ears. She could see yesterday that her cousin's mind was made up. It was like that time when they'd gone for an adventure together and hadn't told any of the grown-ups. Chantal had said she knew the path round the cliff edge was safe and it wouldn't take long.

It had been hours before the sea rescue men had searched the area in their boat and found the two little girls shivering with cold as they'd watched the tide climbing higher up the cliff. They'd had to face the music when their rescuers had taken them home.

Well, Chantal would have to find her own way home this time, wherever that might be, because she'd declared she was definitely returning to Paris, to her own apartment where she would take responsibility for her own future and follow the terms of the legal agreement that she and Michel would draw up. It sounded completely devoid of emotion and intensely hard work. Julia could see it was completely the wrong course of action.

She'd have another try at making Chantal see sense that morning. Glancing at her sleeping husband beside her, she gave a sigh of pure happiness. How could she sell the wonderful idea of marriage and children in a loving marriage to her stubborn cousin? How could she make her realise that anything else would be second best and fraught with problems? Well, that was how she saw it anyway.

Remembering her own doubts and fears before she'd made her lifelong commitment to Bernard she decided she shouldn't be too hard on her cousin. She'd make a start this morning while they were having breakfast together, as they usually did.

As she heard Bernard's mobile buzzing beside the bed she pretended to be asleep, not wanting him to think she'd wasted precious sleeping time on worrying about someone else. She needed all her energy to be devoted to her own welfare and that of the baby, he'd so often told her.

He was speaking in his quiet professional voice now. It sounded urgent. He leaned across. She rubbed her eyes as if coming out of a deep sleep.

'Sorry to wake you, darling, but I've got to go into hospital. Didn't want you to worry where I was. I'll call you later.'

She murmured something vague and turned to face him for his kiss.

As she turned she felt a distinct pain in her lower back. She didn't say anything. Bernard would only start worrying. She was two weeks to her due date now but wouldn't admit to backache until she was sure it was the real thing. It would be much stronger than this, wouldn't it? And there would be other signs before she was convinced. She'd assisted at childbirth on several occasions professionally and had studied numerous textbooks on the subject. But she'd never experienced it herself, had she?

Chantal was sitting by the window in her bedroom, wondering why Julia hadn't arrived this morning. She'd heard Bernard's car leaving earlier as she'd waited for the dawn to break. She'd slept badly because of a real feeling of unhappiness that hung over her. She had to tell Michel the truth today. She had to put on a brave face about it. Make him think she believed this was her only course of action if she was to keep her own integrity.

But if she was truly honest with herself, whenever he was with her she was tempted to take the easy path. Go along with Michel's ideas. Let him make the decisions, as he clearly would like to do. But if she did that she would lose her own identity. She would lay herself wide open to being vulnerable, as she had done with Jacques. She must have been mad to put up with Jacques's whims and fancies! She'd agreed to everything he'd suggested, never queried where he'd been or who he'd been with, welcomed him into her flat with open arms.

Never again, she'd told herself firmly.

It was way past the time that Julia usually arrived. Chantal opened the windows wide to let in the warm sunshine. The sun was high above the top of the hill now. Perhaps Julia was having a lie-in today. Philippe was off on another school trip and had spent the night in a tent and Bernard had left early so who could blame her?

Only two weeks to go now and her cousin was carrying all that extra weight around with her all day. She smiled to herself as she wondered what it would be like towards the end of her own pregnancy with twins.

She would soon know. Time was flying by and she still had so much to organise.

The delicious aroma of hot croissants assailed her nostrils. No need to stay in her room any more. She would spend her last day here checking that she really was getting stronger and was ready to face the outside world and all her problems.

'Come and sit down here, Chantal,' Marianne said, holding back a chair at the long kitchen table. 'I just went in to see Julia but she said she's going to go back to sleep because she had a bad night.'

'Oh, dear! Is she OK?'

'Nothing to worry about, or so she said. I'm going to keep an eye on her all the same. Not long to go now, is it?'

Breakfast over, Chantal had a short stroll in the garden, taking care to walk slowly so as not to tire herself. Yes, she was OK. She increased her speed slightly then paused to smell the scent of the roses, which were beginning to lose their petals. She looked at her watch. There were still a few hours before Michel was due here. She suppressed her feeling of excitement and apprehension. She must stay calm. Stick to her plan. Staying responsible meant no emotion. Completely rational and calm. Easier said than done.

It was now or never! Michel turned the car up the road that led to the farm. Today was the day he was going to take Chantal home. He couldn't wait to have his babies and their mother under his own roof so he could take care of them. He needed to supervise Chantal's prenatal care and make sure she didn't tire herself as she was prone to do.

He'd accepted that he was very fond of Chantal. At times when he was with her it seemed more than just fondness and affection. He found himself listening more to his emotional self and less to his rational self. Chantal had made it clear they should stick to their original plan. She needed her independence. They had to stick to their original plan.

Today he would be totally businesslike—like when he'd tried to persuade her to move into his house. He would say he wanted to show her the new nursery. As soon as they'd known they were expecting twins he'd asked her how she would like the nursery to be fitted out. She'd told him she'd think about it later and let him know.

She still hadn't got back to him so while she'd been here at the farm he'd called in a professional interior design firm. She would be thrilled when she saw the catalogues and designer plans they'd left for them to look though. Such a wide choice of nursery furniture to choose from! Nothing but the best for their twins and their mother.

Michel arrived halfway through the afternoon. Chantal saw his car coming into the farmyard and went to meet him. As long as she was moving around she felt OK. She'd kept herself busy packing her things ready to move out of the room that had been hers for the last couple of weeks.

He was surprised to see her outside. He smiled and kissed her in the French way of greeting a close friend, a kiss on both cheeks. She remained cool, rational, her mind made up. This was how it was going to be.

'Let's go and sit in the conservatory.' She was leading the way round to the front of the farmhouse.

He looked surprised at her suggestion. He'd hoped she would be impatient to be off. 'I hope you're not tiring yourself, Chantal. Wouldn't you like me to help you pack?'

'Marianne helped me this morning. I haven't seen Julia yet today. She was sleeping all morning apparently. Marianne said she'll be down soon to say goodbye.'

As Chantal sank down into one of the squashy armchairs she felt a sudden moment of panic. Michel looked so handsome today in the well-cut grey suit she particularly liked. He looked every inch the successful consultant. He looked like a man who had everything to live for. A good career and in a few months he would be the father of two children. They would be model parents, always putting the needs of their children first.

She took a deep breath. Would that be enough for her? Was she simply running away from having to face her confused emotions every day?

'Michel?'

'Chantal?'

They smiled at each other as they both began to speak at the same time.

'You go first,' he told her.

'No, your turn I think.' She looked directly into his eyes, trying to make sense of that enigmatic expression.

'We need to talk about our immediate plans.'

His serious tone, his nervous expression alarmed her. 'Michel, before you say any more...'

Michel shook his head as she tried to interrupt.

'No, you asked me to speak first. This is really important. I've asked you on several occasions if you will move into my house. It would be safer for the welfare of our babies and much better for your prenatal care and also, if I'm honest, for my peace of mind to have you under my roof. I'm begging you now to reconsider.'

She couldn't speak as she looked at the absolute sincerity in his expression. Tears sprang to her eyes and began to trickle down her cheek at the thought of what she had to do.

Mistaking her reaction, he drew her into his arms.

'Chantal, please say something. Please?'

'Michel I'm going back to my apartment in Paris.'

He looked stunned as she withdrew from his embrace.

'That's what I was going to tell you. I'm carrying your babies and I'm truly committed to the plan we agreed on when we embarked on our parenthood journey together but I've had time to think it through. Too much has happened to me in a short space of time. I can't commit to living under your roof. I need to be totally in charge of my own destiny.'

She dabbed her eyes with a tissue. 'I'm sticking to our original agreement as regards our parenting but that hadn't stipulated moving in with you. I need my own space, my own—'

She broke off as she heard a scream coming from the house. They both stood up as their medical training urged them to go and check out what was happening to Julia.

Marianne was hurrying out through the French windows. 'Julia needs you. You're both doctors so you'll know what to do. She's definitely having strong labour pains now.'

'I'll get Bernard back from the hospital,' Michel said, speaking into his mobile as he hurried into the house. 'Bernard…'

Julia was half sitting, half lying on her bed, doubled up in pain and desperately trying to control her deep breathing.

As the contraction passed Chantal got her to lie down so she could examine her.

'The cervix is well dilated, Julia, but don't start pushing until I tell you.'

Michel had spied a gas and air machine in the corner of the bedroom. Trust Bernard to be prepared at this stage of the pregnancy! He checked the apparatus out before handing Julia the mask.

'There's another contraction coming,' Chantal told her cousin.

'I know, I can feel it! Agh…'

'Breathe into the mask, Julia,' Michel told her as he held it in place.

Minutes later Bernard arrived.

'Darling, hang on in there. You're absolutely brilliant. Yes, keep panting like that. I was driving home when Michel called me. The ambulance will be here as soon as they can get out of the hospital forecourt. There's a traffic jam causing congestion on the seafront.'

Both men had taken off their jackets and rolled up their sleeves and were assessing the dilatation of the cervix. Chantal held tightly to Julia's hand, mopping her brow as the sweat poured from her.

'Don't leave me, Chantal. There's another pain coming.'

'You can push on this one, Julia,' Michel told her. 'OK, that's good, yes, and again.'

'Hold back, Julia,' Michel instructed as he took the baby's head in his hands minutes later.

Bernard was holding his wife now as the baby made his appearance.

'A gentle push now, Julia, and baby will be with us,' Michel told her.

The baby flopped out into his hands and the welcome

sound of his first cry could be heard by everybody. So could their sighs of relief at the safe delivery of this much-wanted son.

Chantal looked across at Michel. She had no idea what he was thinking now as he busied himself cutting the cord, checking the baby's airways. He was behaving as if they were in hospital, as if they were an obstetrics team called in to deliver a patient's baby.

She was glad he was totally calm because she was afraid she was going to pieces. She remembered her cold response to his suggestion that she move in with him. She'd made it quite clear that this would never happen. That must have hurt him enormously. And she also remembered the plans she'd set in motion during the last couple of days. She had to stick to them.

Marianne appeared at the door and was allowed in to see the new baby. 'Oh, he's wonderful. So like Bernard, don't you think, Julia?'

Marianne broke off as she remembered the important message she had to give to Chantal immediately.

'Your car is here, Chantal. The chauffeur says he's taking you to your clinic in Paris. There's a nurse who came with the chauffeur, waiting to help you. Shall I bring her upstairs?'

Chantal swallowed hard. This was what she'd been going to tell Michel just before he'd asked her to move into his house. She'd been in contact with Sebastian and he'd arranged to admit her to his clinic for a check-up before she went to her Paris apartment. He wanted to give her a thorough examination and also make sure that she knew exactly how she was going to prepare for the birth of her twins.

The ambulance had arrived now and staff from the Hôpital de la Plage were now coming up the stairs to take Julia and her baby .

Holding her new baby close to her, Julia was the happiest woman in the world. She only had eyes for her husband and son as medical staff milled around the room, making preparations for their departure.

The nurse from Paris was standing beside Chantal, asking for her suitcase to carry down to the car. The chauffeur had also come upstairs and was waiting in the doorway. Chantal managed to find a way through to Michel.

'Michel, this isn't how I meant it to be. I was going to explain that I need—'

'It's not about what you need now, Chantal,' he told her coldly. 'It's what the twins will require in the future. Make sure you employ a good lawyer to legalise our situation while you're in Paris. That's what you want, isn't it?'

As she sat in the back of the car she knew she would never forget the expression on Michel's face. He'd looked like a man who'd been totally betrayed. Well, in a way he had. She thought of all the times she'd needed him and he'd been there for her. She would never forget that hard expression in his eyes as she'd left him.

The clinic nurse was sitting in front with the driver, occasionally turning round to check that her patient was OK.

'Try to get some rest on the journey,' Chantal had been told.

Rest? Would she ever get rest again from the guilt she was feeling at turning down Michel's well-meant and obviously sensible idea that she should be under his roof with their precious babies. He'd opened up to her and she'd turned him down flat.

And his parting words still rang in her ears. He'd told her she should be thinking about what was best for their babies.

After the birth she'd been caught up in the euphoria surrounding Bernard and Julia as their first baby together arrived safely. That was what a conventional partnership was all about. Would this unconventional plan really work?

CHAPTER FOURTEEN

'PHYSICALLY, YOU'RE IN good shape again.'

Sebastian looked up from the notes on his desk, his eyes taking in Chantal's desperately worried expression. She'd been like this, only more so, when she'd arrived yesterday evening. The nurse who'd accompanied her to the clinic last night had said her patient had appeared to sleep for most of the way until the chauffeur had slowed down to allow for the traffic congestion in Paris. At that point Chantal had woken to look out of the window.

Chantal breathed a sigh of relief at Sebastian's words. 'In that case, I could go back to my apartment, couldn't I, Sebastian?'

'Chantal, you're free to come and go as you please. You and your mother live quite near, so I expect to see you frequently before the babies are born. Is your mother back from holiday yet?'

'Yes, I'll phone her shortly to say I'm coming back today. She knows I'll be back some time this week but I wanted to be sure I checked with you first that all was well.'

'Well, as I said before, you're physically fine again.' He hesitated. 'I'm not sure about your emotional state. Are you sure you can cope with this unorthodox situation you and Michel have created for yourselves?'

Trust Sebastian to hit the nail on the head! He knew her too well.

'I'm not at all sure,' she admitted tentatively. 'But I'm going to give it a good try.'

'Yes, but is it what's best for the babies? You and Michel seem like an ideal couple when you're together. Nobody would know that there wasn't a loving bond between you.'

'Please, Sebastian! It's not as simple as you think. We've both got emotional baggage from the past that prevents us from committing to each other.'

'Chantal, I honestly think you should go and see your mother now. Brigitte's the one who should be advising you, not me. Family is always best in discussions of this nature. I'll give you just one piece of advice, if I may. If there's any chance at all of you having a conventional loving partnership where you commit to each other for life, you must take it.'

Walking down the Rue de l'Assomption towards her apartment block, she could feel butterflies in her tummy. The thought of explaining to her mother everything that had happened to her while she'd been on holiday was making her feel very apprehensive.

Sebastian had reminded her when she'd been leaving the clinic that her mother was a strong, dependable lady. She would take it all in her stride, as she always has done.

She'd nodded in agreement before saying, 'That was why I knew it was possible to give the babies a happy future. I saw how my mother coped by herself.'

'Your mother always gave the impression it was easy,' he'd replied. 'But that was because she didn't want to worry you.'

She stopped walking now to reach for the bleeping mobile in her bag.

'Maman!'

'Chantal, I've just got your message about coming home. That's wonderful. Where are you now?'

'Practically home. I stayed with a friend last night.'

'You should have told me you were here in Paris. I would have…'

Her mother was still talking as Chantal entered the apartment building. The concierge came to meet her, taking control of her trolley case while giving her an effusive welcome. He came with her in the lift, taking her right to her own door before leaving.

Her mother was standing in her own open doorway. They hugged each other.

'It's so good to see you again, Maman. How was the holiday?'

'Come in, come in and let's catch up.'

She followed her mother into her kitchen and sat down at the table.

They drank coffee together, her mother still recounting how wonderful her holiday had been. Chantal was more than happy to simply hear about the sun, the sea, the wonderful restaurants.

'I've eaten far too much during my holiday. I've put on two kilos so I'm going to be careful of my diet until I'm back to normal or none of my clothes will fit me. I had to buy this new blouse. Do you think it—?'

Her mother stopped in mid-flow as she looked across the table.

'You look well,' she said carefully. 'You seem to have put on a bit of weight yourself since I last saw you.'

She waited for her daughter to say something.

Chantal took a deep breath. 'I'm pregnant, Maman.'

'Congratulations, *chérie*! Well, you have been busy while I was away. Are you in a relationship, then?'

'It's rather unconventional, actually.'

'Don't worry. I'm totally unshockable. How unconventional is it.?'

'Well, the father of my babies is...'

'So it's a multiple birth?'

'Just twins, Maman.'

'Fine.' Brigitte reached for the coffee pot and refilled their cups while waiting for her daughter to continue with her unexpected news. She told herself to stay calm. All would be revealed sooner or later and while she was delighted at the thought of being a grandmother she wasn't so sure about the 'unconventional' side of things. But whatever it was, Chantal would have her full support.

'Do you know the sex of your babies?' Brigitte took a sip of her coffee.

'No. My obstetrician asked if I wanted to know but I told him I thought I should allow the babies' father to accompany me to the obstetrician's when their sex is revealed. You see, Maman, I have to be very careful to involve him at important stages of my prenatal and postnatal treatment. We haven't drawn up a legal document yet...'

'So you're going to draw up a legal document?' Whatever next!

Chantal paused, cleared her throat, looked down at her hands and still it was difficult to actually find the right words.

'You see, Michel and I are colleagues—well, actually he's Director of Emergency, which, as you know, is the department I'm working in, so technically he's my boss. We became friends and went out for a meal together.

We sort of found ourselves discussing how we'd always wanted to be parents but that it wasn't possible now.'

Brigitte nodded. She was beginning to guess what was coming.

'It turned out that Michel's wife had died and, well, you know what happened with Jacques. So we agreed to try for a baby together. The idea of a committed relationship didn't come into it. We agreed we would go to a clinic for artificial insemination where Michel would provide the sperm and I would carry the baby but...'

She paused for breath.

'Can you slow down a bit, dear? I think I'm with you so far. Just give me a moment to digest this bit. Don't worry, I've read about AID. So you actually went ahead with this, did you?'

Chantal knew she mustn't show weakness at this point. She must stay firm, she told herself as she searched her handbag for a tissue and blew her nose.

'Well, in the intervening weeks, as we slowly got to know one another better, the dynamic between us changed slightly. Michel decided we should have a meeting at his house to discuss the unconventional partnership we were going to enter into.'

'And...?'

At this point Brigitte had a good idea what might have happened. The way that her daughter was speaking about this doctor called Michel indicated that she had the highest regard for him. Human nature being what it was...

'Well, when we went to his house that evening we were just good friends, discussing an unconventional situation that could work out for both of us.' She paused.

Brigitte couldn't wait to hear what happened. 'So, you both got together that night did you?'

'Mum! How did you know?'

'Chantal, I wasn't born yesterday. It was bound to happen. Two friends wanting a baby. Much better to do it the natural way.'

'But we didn't mean it to happen. We just sort of got carried away and then…well, in the course of one night together…'

She had to stop again. She found herself blushing as the memories of their lovemaking flooded back.

Brigitte smiled. 'I gather you and Michel enjoyed yourselves on the night your babies were conceived?'

'Yes, we did. But we were both intent on keeping to the plan we'd initially made that we should have an un-committed relationship. Good parents but keeping our own independence.'

'Just a moment, Chantal. You didn't think you could honestly do that, did you? Not after you'd made love?'

'Yes, we did think the plan would still work. And at first it did. But as soon as my pregnancy was confirmed I found myself in the middle of a maelstrom of emotional changes that I found difficult to deal with. Then a few weeks ago I had some bleeding, which seemed to signify that I was miscarrying. Thank heavens my babies are still safe!'

'Exactly! Thank goodness the babies are still safe. That's the main thing. I have to say you hit the nail on the head when you said you've been in the middle of a maelstrom of emotional changes. You've had to deal with hormonal changes and from a personal point of view you've had to come to terms with the reaction of your babies' father. How did Michel react when it seemed as if you might lose the babies?'

'He was desperately worried. He'd become very con-cerned about the babies' welfare as soon as he saw them on screen at the first scan. It was almost as if he'd fallen in love with them. And he transferred that concern to me because I was carrying them. He became possessive, always suggesting I should take care when I was working, stop for a proper break at lunchtime…'

'Well, of course he did. And quite right too. I like the sound of this young man.'

'Well, yes, he did care about us a lot, the babies and me. Then he asked me several times to move in with him so he could take care of us. He has this magnificent house on the top of the hill overlooking the bay of St Martin. You know where I mean, Maman? Right at the top before the road goes down the other side.'

'Yes, yes, I know where you mean. I was driving over there last year on my way to Montreuil. I think it was built a couple of years ago. It's a beautiful house and what a view! So when are you moving in?'

'Well, I said I'd think about it. He asked me again yesterday.'

'Yesterday? And you…?'

'It was just before Julia gave birth and we became involved in delivering her baby. She's had a little boy, Maman.'

'But that's wonderful! She must be over the moon. I must phone my sister to congratulate her on becoming a grandmother.'

Brigitte couldn't help wishing Chantal was settled like her niece with a good man by her side. This man Michel could well be the one for her even though she didn't seem to have realised it yet.

'Now, to get back to your unconventional situation, Chantal. After Michel had asked you about moving in and you'd helped to deliver Julia's baby, what was your answer?'

'I said no again and this time I made it clear it was

final. I need to keep my independence. After Jacques deceived me and caused me to miscarry I vowed I would never trust another man.'

'I know you said that then, my love, but circumstances change. I was away on holiday when it all happened and you coped all by yourself. Didn't tell me a thing till weeks afterwards. You try to be too independent. Always have done. Just like your father.'

Brigitte was watching her daughter carefully as she spoke again.

'Chantal, tell me exactly why you can't marry the father of your babies?'

Chantal glared at her mother. 'Because he hasn't asked me, for a start, and if he did? Well, he just won't. He's still in love with his dead wife. I can't compete with a ghost, can I?'

'Ah, so you have thought about it, then?'

'Well, of course I've thought about it but that's as far as it got.'

'If he did ask you to marry him rather than just move in with him would you?'

'Mum, I need to be independent. As I told you, Jacques's deceit triggered my miscarriage. Not only did I lose my baby but I lost the ability to love. As I lay on my bathroom floor in the throes of my miscarriage I remember feeling a change come over me. It felt liberating at the time as I vowed never to commit myself to another man. I knew that would ensure I would never be vulnerable again.'

'But Michel sounds totally different from Jacques. Surely you can see that?'

Chantal could feel tears threatening to roll down her cheeks and remove the hard exterior of herself that she had just tried to portray.

'Yes, I can see that,' she said quietly. 'And that's the problem. The more I fight the feelings I have for Michel, the more I want him, not just because he's the father of my babies but because…because I think…well, I'm sure now that…I love him.'

She choked on her words, desperately reaching again for a tissue.

Brigitte took a box of tissues from a nearby shelf and handed it to her before sitting down again and waiting silently. She felt she'd said enough to bring Chantal to her senses. She mustn't be seen as a nagging mother. She longed to cradle her daughter in her arms as she used to do when Chantal had cried as a child. But she was a big girl now and had to make her own decisions.

She knew she'd needed to break down that icy exterior her daughter had built around herself since she'd been so badly hurt last year by that scoundrel. It had taken a good, thoughtful man like Michel to thaw her out. And it had taken her own tried and tested method of getting through to her daughter's inner self. Chantal had trusted her with the secret she hadn't even admitted to herself.

Her eyes were dry now. 'Mum, I know you think that marriage and a loving, lifelong commitment to a partner are best for a family but you managed alone brilliantly.'

'Chantal, I had no choice! I *had* to make a success of my parenting when your father died. I hadn't *chosen* to be by myself, bringing up a child on my own. Many a night I cried myself to sleep, wishing my wonderful husband was still with me. But I had to keep strong for both of us.'

Chantal reached across the table and squeezed her mother's hand. 'I never knew,' she breathed. 'You always appeared to have everything under control.'

Brigitte wiped a tissue over her own eyes now. 'My advice is go back and find out if Michel would still like you to move in with him. If he does, tell him you will. When you're both under one roof and have babies to care for, love will blossom. I'm sure of it. And when he asks you to marry him…'

'If he asks me to marry him.'

'OK, if he asks you to marry him be sure to say yes. Love and marriage go together. I should know. Those few years I had with your father before he died were the most wonderful, the most…'

They were both reaching for the tissue box now.

'Mum, don't you think it's too late for me to go back to Michel and tell him I've changed my mind about moving in?'

'It's never too late to change your mind. Especially if you're a woman. We're well known for it. But you'll have to grovel.' She gave her daughter a conspiratorial grin.

'Grovel? What do you mean?'

'Eat humble pie, tell him you got it all wrong. Men like to be told that they were right all along. But the important thing is that you tell him. If you do manage to convince him you've changed your mind about moving in with him then you can rest assured that it's quite safe for you to let nature take its course. If you keep an open mind about the situation once you're under his roof, he'll come round to thinking about marriage. He'll find he can't resist making love to you when you're living together and—'

'You really think so?'

'He's a man, isn't he? You're an attractive young woman who's carrying his babies. Your pregnancy is well established now and making love will help to ease the tension between you. Make the first move if you have to. Believe me, he'll love you for it.'

Chantal looked out of the car window at the view of the sea sparkling in the glowing twilight. Before she'd left her mother's apartment she'd phoned Sebastian to tell him she'd changed her mind and was going back to see Michel. He'd insisted on sending his chauffeur to drive her, saying it would be much better she didn't tire herself on the journey.

It had only been as Sebastian's chauffeur had driven off the motorway that led to St Martin sur Mer that she'd phoned Michel to find out where he was. Her mobile had rung for a long time before he'd answered. He had probably been deciding whether to take her call or not.

When he'd finally answered he had been brisk and to the point. He was at home. 'Why do you want to see me?'

'I just need to see you.'

'Well, OK. But make it soon because I have to go out tonight.' He cut the connection.

Predictable reaction, Chantal thought nervously as the car climbed higher up the hill. How long did she need to convince him she'd changed her mind for ever?

The chauffeur lifted her case out of the boot and waited by the door. Butterflies were once again fluttering around in her tummy. The chauffeur had already opened the car door but she remained in her seat watching, watching and planning what to say.

The front door of the house opened.

Slowly, she got out of the car.

Michel, towel in hand, was in his dressing gown, his dark hair wet and rumpled from the shower. He pushed it back from his forehead and took the case from the chauffeur, who returned to the car and started the engine. He'd already told Chantal that Sebastian had asked him to return to Paris that evening.

As the car drove away she felt very apprehensive. Michel's cold manner was scary. She'd never seen him like this before.

She followed him into the house. He dumped her case by the door and went through to the veranda. He stood by the rail of the veranda, looking out at the view, his arms folded, his back towards her.

'I thought you would still be in Paris. If you've got the name of your law firm I'll give them a call in the morning but right now I have to—'

'We need to talk,' she said quietly as she sat down on the nearby sofa. 'I stayed at the clinic last night. Sebastian gave me a full examination today. I had a scan this morning.'

He swung round and moved to her side, looking down at her with an enigmatic expression.

'How are the babies?'

'They're fine. Sebastian asked if I wanted to know the sex but I said I would like you to be with me when we found out—if you do want to find out. It would be the right thing to do and... Oh, Michel, I've changed my mind about moving in here. If you still want me here under your roof I'd love to make this my home while I'm waiting for the babies.'

She'd hoped to control her tears this time to give him a rational explanation in words but possibly her tears would convey her feelings.

'I was wrong, I was so wrong,' she managed to say. 'Can you ever forgive me for being so difficult when you were so kind?'

He sank down beside her and drew her into his arms.

'There's nothing to forgive, he whispered. 'You're carrying my babies, that's enough.'

'No, you deserve more from me, Michel. More commitment to your needs as well as mine.'

His arms tightened around her. 'Chantal, I thought I could never love again but I was wrong. I've been trying to ignore my feelings for you. Trying hard not to fall in love with you. Yes, I'll always love Maxine but my heart is big enough to love both of you. If only you loved me back I would be the happiest man on earth.'

'But I do love you, Michel! I was also trying hard to ignore my feelings for you and pretend I wasn't—'

His lips on hers prevented her from saying anything further.

'Words aren't enough to pledge our love,' he murmured as he scooped her up into his arms and carried her upstairs.'

There was moonlight streaming through the open windows when she awoke. The first thought that occurred to her was that she was home at last, her real home with Michel. She'd never felt happier.

As if sensing that she was looking at him, he opened his eyes.

'You're still here. I thought I might have dreamt it all. If we've conceived two more babies it's going to be a bit crowded in there.'

He placed his hand over her tummy. 'No, I'm confident there's only two in there. I can hear them asking when they can go to sleep again.'

She gave a sigh of happiness. 'It's taken too long for me to admit I was in love with you. The main reason I fought against my true feelings for you is that when I miscarried my first baby last September I vowed I would never trust myself to a man again. Jacques's deception hurt me so much.'

He drew her into his arms. 'Tell me about it,' he said gently. 'I want to know everything about what happened to you.'

She took a deep breath as the awful memories came flooding back. 'Jacques's wife turned up at my flat. I had no idea he was married. I was carrying his baby. I wanted that baby so much. I wanted to be a mother...well, anyway, there was a lot of shouting between them. Apparently that wasn't the first time he'd betrayed her. Finally the shouting stopped and they left together.'

She snuggled close to Michel. He was stroking her hair. She felt safe in his arms.

'Please go on, darling. I need to know if I'm to understand what changed you.'

'I began to feel ill. I thought it was simply the horrible experience I'd just been through. I told myself I was strong enough to forget his deception and move on. I would give my unborn baby all the love I was capable of. My mother had brought me up by herself after my father died so I could do the same.'

She broke off to compose herself again. 'I didn't realise it had triggered a miscarriage. When I found myself on the bathroom floor, doubled up in pain, I felt a change coming over me. I became hard. I vowed that no man would ever cause me such pain and anguish again.'

He kissed her gently on the cheek. 'My poor darling. I can see now why you were wary of commitment. You thought all men were the same, didn't you?'

'Until I met you,' she whispered, looking up into his eyes where she could see her own love mirrored there.

She moved in his arms as she felt desire mounting between them. His lips were on hers. She welcomed the gentle feel of his kiss, the sensual, exciting touch of his hands exploring her body. They blended together, making love once more until they climaxed together, both of them knowing that their love for each other would last for ever. Nothing could break the bond between them.

Chantal came round from her sensual snooze in Michel's arms. She looked up at him and saw he was wide awake, his eyes dreamy and loving as he returned her gaze.

'Michel, you forgot you were going out, didn't you? Will someone be waiting for you?'

'Ah, yes, my mythical date. Pure fantasy. Nothing wrong with that when you're still hurting from the fact that the mother of your babies has refused to move in with you. But I'll forgive you now I understand the reasons behind your desire to remain totally independent of any man after your horrible experience with Jacques.'

'And I'm relieved you've realised it's possible to love Maxine at the same time as you're loving me.'

'Only you could have made me realise that,' he murmured.

She smiled up at him. 'And only you could have made me fall in love again.'

His lips brushed hers. 'If I were to say four little words to you, would you give me an answer?'

'That depends on what the little words are. Please don't keep me in suspense.'

'Tradition requires me to get out of bed and go down on one knee.'

She remained silent. She would remember these precious moments for the rest of her life, she knew.

He was looking up at her from the side of the bed, gazing at her with such love that she thought her heart would burst.

'Will you marry me?'

He held out his hands towards her. As she clasped them she felt a shiver going down her spine. She'd been utterly transformed since they'd both confessed their love for each other.

'Yes, oh, yes, of course I will. Michel, I love you so much I…'

He was holding her in his arms again, covering her face with kisses as they vowed they would love each other for the rest of their lives.

He knew that he would never forget how beautiful his bride-to-be looked when she agreed to marry him.

EPILOGUE

As Chantal and Michel changed their twins' nappies in the nursery they could hear the sound of their guests arriving downstairs and in the garden. They'd chosen to wait until the babies were four months old before having an official party to publicly celebrate their wedding and the birth of their babies.

They'd had a wonderfully quiet, low key wedding in October at the church in Montreuil for close family and friends but today was a big event where they were going to show off their babies.

Chantal looked up at Michel and smiled. 'What a difference a year makes!'

He laughed. 'Any regrets?'

'You must be joking. Last June I was still agonising about the past and the effect it had had on me. Today I'm the happiest woman alive. Mother of two, wife of the most wonderful—'

'Oh, spare my blushes, Chantal! When you've finished with that nappy bin on your side of the cots, could you pass it this way? Eugh! What a stink!'

Chantal laughed. 'You can be so romantic, Michel.'

He dropped the bin on the floor and drew her into his arms. 'If it's romance you want, darling, you've come to the right man. I was just wondering if we've time to...'

A loud wailing sound came from both cots.

'Michel, they're both hungry, remember.'

He kissed her on the cheek and released her. 'OK. Later. You take Rose, I'll deal with Christophe.'

They settled themselves in the comfortable feeding chairs by the French doors that led onto the balcony, from where they could see their guests arriving. The perfume from the roses wafted up from the garden.

Chantal looked down at her little daughter who was sucking noisily on her bottle. The little blue eyes gazed trustingly back at her. Had she ever imagined a year ago that she would be as blessed as she was now? And to be a mother with a boy and a girl. This was where she truly belonged. They were a real family.

Someone was tapping on the door.

Michel looked up from baby Christophe. *'Entrez!'*

Angeline, who helped them with the babies and some of the housekeeping, came in.

'Chantal, would you like me to take over the feeding for you? The caterers are setting out the lunch buffet in the marquee and I've got time to help you now.'

'Good. You can take Christophe.' Michel stood up, cradling his son, and handed him over to Angeline. 'I'll go and change.'

Chantal smiled at Angeline as she settled herself in the seat that Michel had just vacated. Angeline had proved to be a brilliant addition to the household. She'd had nursery training but was also happy to help around the house and turn her hand to anything that needed to be done. A distant relative of Marianne, Julia's housekeeper, she was exactly what they needed.

Chantal hadn't wanted to keep on the obstetric nurse they'd employed for the first month of the twins' lives. She'd wanted to be a hands-on mum, taking care of her own babies. And she found that she was in no hurry to return to her medical career. Being a full-time mother was all she'd ever dreamed of. Especially when Michel was happy to help her whenever he wasn't on duty at the hospital.

She could hear the hum of conversation downstairs. Rose took her little rosebud lips from the bottle and looked up at her mother as if to say she didn't want any more. The bottle was almost empty.

She lifted her daughter over her shoulder, rubbing her back gently until she heard and felt the reassuring burp that told her Rose had been winded.

'I'll put Rose in the playpen for a few minutes, Angeline. Christophe can join her when he's finished feeding.'

It had only taken her a few minutes to change into the cool white linen skirt and jacket she'd chosen for the occasion. With her hand on the banister as she hurried downstairs, she paused for a moment to look at the friends, relatives and medical colleagues chatting to each other in the large entrance hall.

'Chantal!' Pierre Marchand, the obstetric consultant who'd been such a help during her pregnancy, called out. 'You look wonderful! Nobody would think you were the mother of two babies.'

She smiled as she continued down the stairs.

'Who's looking after the shop today?' she asked her medical colleagues as she was warmly welcomed into the group. 'So many of you are here today! Thank you all for coming. I hope we don't get an emergency.'

A chorus of agreement rang out as she passed through the hall, saying a few words to everybody before going out into the garden.

The marquee on the lawn was also crowded with

friends, relatives and a large number of medical colleagues. Chantal again found herself hoping there wouldn't be a major disaster that would send them all scurrying back to the hospital. She noticed many of her colleagues were drinking fruit juice or fizzy water just in case.

The caterers had set out an excellent buffet at the far end of the marquee and guests were wandering outside in the garden, enjoying the summer morning.

Michel came across from the group he was entertaining when he saw his wife. 'You look wonderful,' he whispered. 'Everybody's asking to see the babies. Shall we go and bring them out here before it gets too hot?'

She nodded in agreement as he took her hand and led her back up the stairs. In the nursery their babies were kicking their legs in the playpen. Chantal had laid out their clothes on the bed. That was supposed to be her own bed but she preferred to sleep in the next room with Michel, leaving the adjoining room door open. Consequently, 'her' bed acted as a dressing space for the twins' clothes.

'Shall I help you, Chantal?' Angeline was already lifting baby Rose from the playpen.

Michel lifted out Christophe but handed him to Chantal. 'I'm no good with buttons and zips.'

He watched as his babies were decked out in the beautiful garments Chantal had chosen for their public appearance today. The babies were wearing little white two-piece outfits, a dress for Rose and trousers for Christophe.

Chantal took the baby hairbrush and passed it gently over their soft blond hair. Gently she gathered Rose into her arms and Michel picked up Christophe. Together they went down the stairs. The people in the hall gave a collective sigh as they appeared. 'Oh, look at the babies! Aren't they gorgeous? What a beautiful picture they make as a family.'

They made their way slowly through the admiring crowd, out into the garden where there were more 'oohs' and 'ahs' of appreciation.

Sebastian and Susanna gave their approval at the brilliant progress of the babies.

'Thank you so much for all your help during the pregnancy,' Chantal whispered to Sebastian.

'It was an absolute pleasure to see the outcome, Chantal. Thank goodness it's all been such a success. May you have a long and happy family life together. I know you've got a ready-made family with your boy and girl but are there any plans to enlarge it in the future? You're both completely natural parents.'

'Oh, yes, we've got plans,' Michel told Sebastian.

'Glad to hear it,' Susanna said.

'Chantal!' Julia, followed by Bernard and the boys, came hurrying across the lawn. The two cousins were soon catching up on everything that had happened in the last few days since they'd last seen each other. Philippe was carrying his baby half-brother Thibault and showing him his baby cousins.

'They're our second cousins,' he was saying in a serious voice, as if his eight-month-old brother knew what he was talking about. 'You see, our mother is Chantal's first cousin so...' He glanced up at his father. 'Do you think Thibault understands what I'm saying, Papa?'

Bernard nodded gravely. 'Of course. Like you, he's very bright for his age.'

Chantal moved on to the seat under the trees where she'd spotted her mother deep in conversation with her twin. It was obvious that Brigitte and Berenice were trying to catch up with their news as she and Julia had just done.

Both sisters turned at the sound of Chantal's voice and they both insisted on holding the babies. Brigitte took Rose into her arms. Michel followed shortly with Christophe and handed him over to his great-aunt Berenice.

The sisters were besotted with the babies. 'You can leave them with us,' Brigitte said. 'Go off and talk to your guests. We'll take care of them. Don't hurry back.'

'Come and have a look at the roses with me,' Michel said as he took Chantal's hand.

She knew exactly where he was taking her. They'd been here many times before. There was a secret garden, which was difficult to find unless you knew it was there. They went through the ivy-clad archway and were finally alone.

'I just had to have you all to myself for a few minutes.' He drew her into his arms. 'You look absolutely radiant.'

As she responded to his kiss she reflected that they were going to be together for the rest of their lives but she would always remember this special moment. They were a real family now but there was still romance in their lives, always would be.

'This is where they are!'

A whole crowd of colleagues from the hospital staff had joined them, followed by the wine waiters, who were topping up their glasses.

'Here's to the happy couple! May all your troubles be little ones.'

She recognised the English voice of her eldest cousin,

who was a consultant in a London hospital. He was Julia's elder brother.

'Congratulations on the birth of your twins!' Everyone was joining in the toast, raising their glasses.

'I was so happy when I saw the twins on the screen after your threatened miscarriage,' said Pierre Marchand, the obstetrics consultant at the Hôpital de la Plage who, in liaison with Sebastian in Paris, had seen Chantal through her pregnancy. He also raised his glass. 'I'm so glad we didn't lose them. Chantal, you were a brilliant patient at that difficult time. You did everything I told you to and look at you now, positively blooming with good health!'

'To the twins?' Genevieve from Obstetrics lifted her glass for another top-up. That definitely calls for another toast. You're not on call, Pierre, are you? Well, thank goodness for that!'

'Speech!'

Michel rose to the occasion, welcoming everyone, paying compliments to his beautiful wife, his wonderful babies, saying thank you to everyone who'd helped during the pregnancy. Everyone cheered as he swiftly brought the impromptu speech to its conclusion.

Sensing the demand for further speeches would arrive as the champagne flowed, he put his arm round Chantal and guided her away from their no-longer-secret garden. Grandmother Brigitte and Great-Aunt Berenice had waved them away when they'd returned to claim their babies, telling them they needed more time with the little darlings.

Their guests were milling round the buffet now. The band had arrived and was in place on the lawn, playing music for dancing. Michel took her in his arms and guided her round the lawn in a slow foxtrot. Everybody

cheered as they finished. Chantal knew she would remember this day for the rest of her life.

'Have the guests all gone now?' Michel asked when Angeline came to help them settle the babies.

Angeline nodded. 'The last taxi of guests has just
driven off and my taxi is on its way up the hill. Thank
you for ordering it for me, Michel.'

'Thank you for all your help. The babies are both
asleep, as you can see,' he whispered. 'That sounds like
your taxi in the drive now. Goodnight, Angeline.'

They were alone at last. Michel took Chantal's hand as
they tiptoed away from the sleeping babies in their cots.
As they went through into their bedroom he unzipped
the strapless blouse beneath her jacket.

'I've been wanting to do that all day.'

'I've been waiting for the time when you could safely
do that all day! Oh, that's better.' She kicked off her kit-
ten-heeled shoes and curled up in an armchair beside
the bed.

'Let me help you into bed, darling.' Gently he lifted
her onto their enormous bed.

'Comfy enough?' He snuggled up to her, struggling to
throw the rest of his clothes away onto the thick carpet.

She turned towards him.

He put out a hand and gently stroked her face. 'How
are you feeling?'

'Fit and healthy. Not a bit tired. Fabulous day, don't
you think? I was so apprehensive this morning about all
the arrangements we'd made.'

'So was I. It went off very well, didn't it? Good planning, Chantal.'

'I was going to say the same to you, Michel. We make
a good team.'

'No planning needed tonight.'

She sighed. 'All night alone together.'

'Apart from our babies.'

'They're snuggled up together side by side just like we are.'

'Well, not exactly…' She snuggled against him as he drew her into his arms. Life couldn't get much better than this.

* * * * *

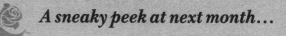

A sneaky peek at next month...

MEDICAL & ROMANCE™

THE ULTIMATE IN ROMANTIC MEDICAL DRAMA

My wish list for next month's titles...

In stores from 7th February 2014:

❑ Tempted by Dr Morales

& The Accidental Romeo — Carol Marinelli

❑ The Honourable Army Doc — Emily Forbes

& A Doctor to Remember — Joanna Neil

❑ Melting the Ice Queen's Heart — Amy Ruttan

& Resisting Her Ex's Touch — Amber McKenzie

Available at WHSmith, Tesco, Asda, Eason, Amazon and Apple

Just can't wait?

Visit us Online

You can buy our books online a month before they hit the shops! **www.millsandboon.co.uk**

0114/03

Join the Mills & Boon Book Club

Subscribe to **Medical** today for 3, 6 or 12 months and you could **save over £40!**

We'll also treat you to these fabulous extras:

 FREE L'Occitane gift set worth £10

 FREE home delivery

 Rewards scheme, exclusive offers…and much more!

Subscribe now and save over £40
www.millsandboon.co.uk/subscribeme